NOBODY'S PERFECT
Douglas Clark

Also available in Perennial Library
by Douglas Clark:

NOBODY'S PERFECT

Douglas Clark

Harper & Row, Publishers
New York, Cambridge, Philadelphia, San Francisco
London, Mexico City, São Paulo, Singapore, Sydney

A hardcover edition of this book was published in England by Cassell & Company Ltd. and in the United States by Stein & Day, Publishers. It is here reprinted by arrangement with the author.

First PERENNIAL LIBRARY edition published 1986.

Library of Congress Cataloging-in-Publication Data

Clark, Douglas.
  Nobody's perfect.

  I. Title.
PR6053.L294N6   1986   823'.914   85-45184
ISBN 0-06-080796-2 (pbk.)

86 87 88 89 90   OPM   10 9 8 7 6 5 4 3 2 1

NOBODY'S PERFECT

1

It was a bright Tuesday morning in October. The ten o'clock sun came unhampered through the wide windows of the new Yard building and cast deep shadows of the handrails on the stairs as Masters and Green tramped down, side by side, in grim silence. Normally Masters would have appreciated the effect. Today, as they set out to investigate the sudden death of Adam Huth he was thinking savagely that this was the fifth successive time he'd been saddled with Green as assistant on a major case. He didn't like the idea that the pairing was becoming accepted as a permanency. He didn't like Green, either, and definitely didn't want a passed-over old has-been tied to his tail forever.

Green's thoughts were equally hostile. Masters had grown too big for his boots. It always happened when young coppers were jammy enough to catch somebody's eye and get promoted too soon.

Masters settled himself heavily in the back seat of the Vauxhall. Green climbed in beside him, still trying to figure out how Masters had managed to claw his way above older and better men. Particularly as Green thought he had no more than an average flair for detection. Yet Masters was looked on as a flier at the Yard. Green felt destructively bitter at the thought of any man getting ahead for reasons other than those of sheer merit and length of service. He leaned back in his corner as far away from Masters as possible and swore to himself he would find some excuse for not working with him again, even if it meant asking for a transfer to one of the Divisions.

The two sergeants, Hill and Brant, were already seated in front.

Masters said: "Take the West Road." Hill started up. "Look out for one of these modern blocks called Barf House. Spelt BARUGT."

"The drug company?"

"Their head office."

The car moved off. Masters took a large-bowled pipe from his breast pocket where he carried it wedged upright by a white silk handkerchief. Green watched the slim hands pack Warlock Flake in the pipe. This was another source of irritation: that so big a man as Masters should have such hands, well-kept and brown-skinned, as though their owner had just returned from a holiday in the sun. They made Green feel socially inferior. When he was a little boy his mother had always told him how important hands were as she treated her own work-worn fingers with cheap glycerine and rosewater each night. Now he supposed he had a complex about them. He associated fine hands with swells—his mother's word—and because of this he felt his own stubby fingers branded him with the indelible stamp of lowly

2

birth. The hell of it was the feeling only came on in Masters' company.

Hill and Brant sensed the atmosphere in the back of the car. They cut out their usual backchat and kept eyes front. Nobody said a word until after the Chiswick roundabout. Then Masters said, "This is the first time I've ever been landed with the chairman of a big company killed in his private office."

"What's different about it?" asked Green.

"I've never had anything to do with big business before."

"It'll be no different from anything else. They'll be humans, won't they?"

"Too many humans. Eight hundred working there by day and probably an army of cleaners at night. Swarming all over the shop. We won't be able to bottle that lot up for questioning."

Green felt a surge of sour pleasure. He could actually taste it at the back of his tongue, like being sick used to be a relief when he'd overeaten as a kid. He thought it was unlike Masters to admit the possibility of difficulties at any time. Yet here he was with the jimjams before they'd even started on this case. Just because it was a bit different from the nice little domestic tragedies he'd tackled so far. For a moment he hoped Masters would fall down on the job.

Masters said: "Adam Huth was *somebody*."

So that's it, thought Green. These nobs are all alike. They even find class distinction in murder. He's actually frightened because the victim's an important man.

Masters went on, "The successful head of one of the most dynamic firms in the country, with big home and export sales."

"And even bigger beautiful profits made out of us poor suckers who pay National Health."

3

"Did you know him?"

"I know he's a big capitalist who's been getting all nosey-botty with a Labour government just to get a knighthood. It makes me want to puke."

"You're suggesting he should come to a sticky end just because he's done his damnedest to support the government's plea for more productivity?"

"That's not what I meant. After you've been in this game as long as I have you'll know that when a creeper like him gets the chop the pressure's put on us from all sides."

"So you think we've got to make sure this time?"

"And be quick about it. The Barugt Company's American-owned." Green said it as though this fact made the task doubly distasteful to him.

"What does nationality matter? You said yourself they'll all be human."

"There'll be pressure just the same. Even if we don't get chased from up top, there'll be executives and vice-presidents, whatever they are, trying to outsmart us."

"When I suggested this a few minutes ago you pooh-poohed the idea."

"I've changed my mind. They'll try to use business jargon to keep us guessing. They're trained that way in Yank firms. Go one better than the next man or get out."

Masters asked: "No union to protect them?" The dig at Green's socialism made him feel better. Like landing a sweet blow in a scrap.

"Have your laugh. You'll soon find out what I mean."

"Goolies! All the employees are British. It's an autonomous company."

"I don't know what that means but I suppose it makes everything just lovely. Even if they are British they'll be like religious maniacs. Converts are more fanatical than those born to it."

4

Masters relit his pipe. He thought Green was trying to be more bloody-minded than ever, and the time was fast approaching when he would have to be taught who was boss.

Green went on, "That's why Yank firms corner the markets over here—after they've taught their business methods. They brainwash the workers." He sounded as if he thought this explanation put his other claims beyond doubt. "We ought to nationalize the lot."

Hill said: "Coming up on the left, sir." He slowed to turn the Vauxhall into the forecourt of Barugt House, stark as a child's building toy on a green tablecloth. A constable posted outside the great glass doors flagged them down.

As soon as they were out of the car Green said with a sneer, "See what I mean?" Masters looked up. Above the doors a green and gold fascia board shouted: "BARUGT HOUSE. ALL WHO LABOUR WITHIN THESE WALLS DO SO IN THE CAUSE OF HUMANITY."

Masters felt sick. He made for the door.

"Detective Chief Inspector Masters?" asked the constable, looking at Green.

"Him," said the older man, jerking a thumb in Masters' direction.

"Superintendent Bale asked me to tell you he's on the tenth floor with the deceased, sir."

"We'll join him there."

"Lift on the right, sir. Self-operating."

Brant pushed the up button. Number-one cage came down and opened its doors.

"Not that lift." The commissionaire was wearing green livery, and standing behind a reception counter. He looked like a retired army man, and sounded as if he'd been severely niggled by some event he didn't like or couldn't understand.

Masters said, "It's going up."

5

The commissionaire glared at the bags the sergeants were carrying. "No cases allowed in that lift. That's for V.I.P.s, and cases and trolleys scratch the paint."

"We promise to be very careful."

"I've told you." The commissionaire came slowly round from behind his desk.

Green and the sergeants stood still. Brant held the retain button. They all knew that Masters' rating of his own importance when he was on the job was as high as Everest. Failure by others to recognize it usually led to a display of temper. Uncharacteristically, Masters kept control. Green thought he'd go to pieces; and in front of a hall porter, at that.

Masters said in his normal voice, "I'm a senior police officer. I go where I like, when I like and how I like. Understood?"

"Have it your way," said the commissionaire. "I've got my orders."

"And you've told us. We'll still take this lift."

Green began to be worried. He thought he knew Masters well enough, but now he was acting out of character. Masters had acted this way on purpose. He didn't want to get het up before they started; and in any case, he thought he quite admired the old commissionaire for standing up to four policemen so stoutly.

"D'you want me to take you up?"

"We'll manage, thank you."

Hill looked about him as the doors closed. "Pretty lush, this, for a lift. If it's anything to go by, we ought to have brought a lawnmower."

Brant asked: "Why?"

"To cut a path through the pile on the carpet to get to the boss's desk."

They stepped out into a vestibule. The wall-to-wall carpet was thick with rubber underlay; and dark green to contrast with the pale pitch-pine panelling. Ahead of them were washrooms and lavatories with the silhouette of a man on one door and a mini-skirted nymph on the other. The doors were flush mahogany with round, flat handles as big as teaplates made of the same wood. Immediately to the right, in line with the lifts, was a single door. Further away, at right angles, were double glass doors giving onto an open plan office. To the left were another two single doors next to each other. One was labelled: "Conference and Board Room," the other: "Mr A. L. Huth, Chairman" and "Miss S. T. Krick, Personal Assistant."

Masters went into the one with Huth's name on it. It was the P.A.'s office, with a uniformed sergeant in occupation.

"Superintendent Bale's in the inner office, sir. He'd like you to go through."

Green followed him. Bale was sandy-haired, with freckles on pale skin. He was lean and long-jawed, with thin lips. He gave the impression of being extremely tall with a slight stoop until Masters approached him. Masters' height, seemingly lessened by his breadth, cut Bale down to size. The superintendent looked undernourished and ailing beside the chief inspector.

Bale said, "Hello. How do you do?" It was a careful, precise voice. Masters thought Bale must have worked hard to cultivate it, because the aitches were slightly too pronounced, as though he were afraid of dropping them. But in spite of the veneer, the voice was warm enough to add sincerity as he went on, "I was interested when the Yard said they were sending *you*. I've heard things about you lately. I want you to do a good job for me here."

Green daren't say "I told you so" but the glance he gave Masters meant he hadn't missed the first pressure.

"I'll do my best," said Masters. "Is this Huth?"

"Admirable Adam or A.A. was what his workers called him," said Bale. "He's not very admirable now."

Huth was lying in a swivel chair which had circular movement and controlled tilting backwards. The weight of the body had set it back so that, though the head was lolling forward, the face was visible to Masters as he stooped to examine it.

Masters said: "He was a distinguished-looking man. Slightly fleshy, perhaps."

The full head of clean grey hair—clean in so far as it was not flecked with still dark strands—was parted very exactly to show a line of pink, shiny scalp. At odds with this, the flesh of the face was greyish blue, the jowls sagging slightly, and there were signs of vomit round the mouth.

Green said, "He looks like Claude Rains to me."

Masters looked up, frowned at the irrelevancy and said, "I want you to find the head of the Personnel Department and go through the records of senior employees who have left at any time since Huth became chairman of Barugt."

"That's more than six years ago," said Bale.

"You want me to find somebody who was fired, and still has a grudge against Huth?"

Masters said, "I don't know whether you'll find one or a hundred, but it's the obvious step to take."

When Green had gone Masters said, "Why murder and not suicide?"

Bale pointed to a small brown bottle on the desk. "He died from poison. That's empty now, but I imagine whatever he took was in it."

"Sounds suspiciously like suicide."

"Meant to look like it, you mean. See the label? Nutidal capsules. Non-poisonous. And Huth would know. It's one of his own drugs."

8

"You're saying the drugs were switched and he took some form of poison by mistake?"

"That's my theory. And my Divisional Surgeon says that his preliminary investigation suggests barbiturate overdosage."

Masters peered again at Huth's face. "The grey skin indicates cyanosis."

"You appear to know all about it."

"Not quite. Did the Surgeon say anything else?"

"He confirmed it by inspecting the mucous membranes. They're blue, too."

"Lack of oxygen again. Do we know when he died?"

"Not to within three or four hours. My information is that he would suffer shock and go into a coma long before the end."

"I seem to remember that barbiturate poisoning lowers the blood pressure and the body temperature. Did that affect your man's assessment? There's central heating on, too."

"He took it all into account."

"What other effects did he say barbiturates have?"

"Respiratory depression," said Bale. "The breathing gets shallow. And there's a lot more, like losing the use of muscles and eyes and so on. Nothing very important."

"I don't agree."

Bale started in surprise. "Why?"

"If he lost the use of his muscles it would explain why he didn't pick up a phone and call for help or why he didn't crawl out of the office."

"I hadn't got as far as thinking about that. But the phone switchboard is closed down at five-thirty and the only one he could have used after that is the commissionaire's in the foyer."

"What's his name?"

"The commissionaire's? Mablethorpe."

"Thanks. So we've got to be satisfied with the fact

9

that he just died sometime during the night?"

"Between midnight and four. The post-mortem might tell you more exactly."

Masters looked about him. As Hill had foreseen, the room was large and palatial. One end was occupied by the desk and usual office accoutrements of a senior executive. The other half was furnished for comfort. A circular table on an extensible central leg could be raised to normal height or lowered as it now was to coffee-table level. It was surrounded by three easy chairs and a long studio couch backed against the end wall. There were two short-shorn sheepskins on the floor, a triangular wine cupboard in one corner, and opposite the windows, a glass-fronted bookcase. Masters strolled over to inspect the titles.

"*The Art of Selling, The Science of Marketing, The Hard Sell, The Soft Sell.* Good lord! There's scores of them. And the next shelf's all advertising. D'you think he'd read them all?"

"He was a very successful businessman."

"More of a businessman than a drug technologist?"

"Naturally. He could hire the brains of technicians and researchers. He exploited their efforts."

"How old was he?"

"Younger than he looked. That grey hair was misleading. He was forty-two."

"Ah!" said Masters, still looking at the books. "A rift in the lute." He opened the glass door and took out one of the volumes. "*After Dinner Stories for Businessmen!*" He looked inside. "Quite fruity, if a little corny. Still, I suppose he could dress them up a bit and make them topical. They'd still be fruity." He replaced the book and turned to Bale. "You still haven't finished telling me why it was murder and not suicide."

Bale said dogmatically: "Huth was a successful man.

10

He was well liked and his firm was flourishing. He was earning as many thousands as we are hundreds. He left no suicide note. He knew about drugs, yet he died slowly, and probably in great discomfort." He shrugged his thin shoulders. "There's a score of reasons why suicide doesn't make sense. I may be wrong, but you'll have to prove it before I'll believe it."

Masters moved over to the windows, noted the feel and quality of the curtains and appreciated the lovely view stretching from the well-kept lawns far below to the distant countryside. "I'll treat it as murder. Have you arranged for the post-mortem?"

"They'll fetch the body whenever you're ready. Give me a ring at the station."

"And the inquest? You'll do that, too, I hope."

"You don't want to be there?"

"What's the point? You can get the finding we want without my help."

There was a silence. Bale lit a cigarette and as an afterthought offered one to Masters who shook his head. "I suppose you're waiting for me to go so that you can get on with it?"

Masters knew Bale would like to stay. But he wanted no superior hampering him and achieving nothing but rebuffs to his own ego. Inspector Green, Masters thought, was enough of a hindrance in any investigation. By his silence he had as good as asked Bale to go. The superintendent had been sensitive enough to take the hint. Masters wasn't going to keep him any longer.

"You've helped a lot," said Masters as they passed together into the P.A.'s office.

Bale said, "Don't butter me up. I'll be surprised if I've saved you five minutes. Call on me for anything you want."

Bale went, taking his sergeant with him. Masters

turned to Hill and Brant. "Everything," he said laconically. It was all they needed. Hill, the fingerprint expert, carried a portable laboratory. Brant was the photographer—among other things—and carried a large amount of equipment. The stuff Mablethorpe hadn't wanted to let into the lift. Between them, Masters knew, they could search a room, find fingerprints, record them, and unearth the trivia of material fact which so often helped him, but the discovery of which he himself found so boring.

Huth's fingerprints were taken, and the body photographed from various angles. The contents of the pockets were lined up on the desk.

"Get him covered," said Masters. "I'll ring for them to fetch him. I've a feeling the body will tell us nothing except the exact poison he took. And I expect there's enough of every sort of dope in this place to kill half London."

Brant went in search of a sheet to cover the corpse. Masters rang Bale.

"These glasses," said Hill, "they've got Huth's prints on them."

"Where did you find them?"

"In the desk cupboard."

"Have they been used for drink?"

"The big one for brandy. The other for sherry, I think. He's got a private store here in the desk." The left-hand pedestal was drawers, the right-hand a cupboard. Hill opened it for Masters to see. The inside of the door had two small brass galleries for holding glasses. The cupboard shelves held the bottles. Hill said, "This was for secret drinking. I expect he kept the cocktail cabinet in the corner for when he had visitors."

"Everything ready to hand," said Masters, squatting with difficulty between the dead man's chair and the

12

cupboard door, which was prevented by a patent check from swinging open more than ninety degrees. "Hennessy, Bristol Milk, Gordon's, Bell's, genuine D.O.M.— just about everything, but only one glass of each type. It begins to look as if our friend was a bit of a toper." He straightened up, red in the face. "When were those two glasses used?"

"My guess is yesterday. They're not dry yet. Look obliquely at where the stems join the bowls. See?"

"Faint brownish marks."

"Refraction of light. The tiniest little drop left will give you that effect."

Brant came in. "Trying to find a sheet in this place is as bad as trying to get Inspector Green to vote for Moseley. First of all I got into trouble for trying to pinch a tablecloth from the directors' dining-room. Would you believe it, they've got a butler down there? Pin-stripe trousers, black waistcoat, and garters round his arms to keep his shirt sleeves up. It's a fact."

"Where did you eventually get the sheet?"

"The women's rest room, Chief. I got some funny looks from a crowd waiting for a lift on the third floor when they saw me coming out of there, I can tell you. I was lucky there wasn't a bit of capurtle in there with the collywobbles, otherwise you'd have had to bail me out. I don't think anybody could get away with much in this place without being spotted."

"I wonder if whoever did this bloke in was seen?" said Hill as he helped spread the sheet over Huth.

"Seen? Or noticed?" asked Masters. "People see but don't notice familiar faces in familiar places. Brant was noticed because everything about him was wrong. Wrong face, wrong sex for that particular room and wrong article to be carrying in this building. By the way, does anybody know where Miss Krick is at the moment?"

"His P.A.?" asked Hill. "She's next door in the conference room. Superintendent Bale put her in there to wait for you."

Masters went through the P.A.'s office and through the connecting door to the boardroom. At the far end of the long, polished table was Huth's personal assistant, typing listlessly. She was copying from a tape on a Grundig recorder. The earphone and voice on the tape prevented her from hearing his approach over the thick carpet. She looked up in surprise when she sensed him towering above her. She took her foot from the control and the headset off.

"Are you a policeman?" She asked without apparent interest, merely for something to say.

"Masters, Scotland Yard," he said, as if giving the question the small attention it deserved. He was watching her face, noting the eyes puffy from weeping, and the droop of the full, petulant lips. He took a seat on the table. She grew uncomfortable at his nearness and the way he stared.

She said: "You'll know me next time, won't you?" It was a pert, defensive little crack that he thought she would never have dreamt of using in different circumstances. The sort of thing she might have said when she was ten years old. By this time he had sized her up, as a sculptor soaks up detail. She wasn't too bad, he thought. Mature in age but immature in appearance. Full cheeks, baby blue eyes made more blue by eye shadow, and hair—too pale to be pure gold—swept up at the back in a tortoise-shell comb. He pigeon-holed her as a pretty-pretty giglet rather than a woman with beauty of character; but, he added to himself, all right for a tumble if you liked them pneumatic.

"How many P.A.s are there in Barugt House?"

It was a habit he had consciously cultivated—to ask

14

a question he knew would be totally unexpected—when he wasn't quite sure how to begin. He felt clever because of it and enjoyed seeing surprise appear on the faces of people he was questioning. This way he felt he got an initial moral ascendancy. He was not disappointed this time. She was taken aback and had to think for a few seconds. "Four. Perhaps five. It's a big company and status changes happen every day. I can't be expected to remember them all."

She was on the defensive. Making excuses for not knowing. He wondered why. When it came to murder, he thought, and you don't know who's done it, and the woman nearest the victim starts making excuses about nothing, there's only one thing to do. Keep asking embarrassing questions and see how she reacts.

"Are they all as good-looking as you, or is the most beautiful reserved for the chairman?"

He thought most modern girls would have accepted it as a compliment, and come back at him with some wisecrack. Krick didn't. She flamed into colour and answered stiffly, "I got my job purely on secretarial merit." It rang true, but thin. She didn't look like somebody who would normally have objected to his question. He felt he was getting warm.

"You've been crying. Why? A girl who's nothing more than an efficient secretary never becomes emotionally involved with her boss, does she? Or does she?"

"I'm sorry Mr Huth is dead. That's all."

"Was he married?"

"Yes."

"Happily?"

She looked down and touched the bar of the typewriter with one finger. "I don't know."

"You must know. Was he so wrapped up in his business he had no time to spare for his home? Did he ever

15

ring his wife from the office? Did she ever ring him? Did he ever talk about family life, or his kids, if he had any?"

"He was a very busy man." Now she was adamant, trying to head him off.

He said, "So his private life was not entirely happy. What happened? Did he look for comfort somewhere else? Were you, by any chance, his mistress?"

Now she was angry. Too angry, he thought. Not a simple denial. In fact, no denial at all. "I don't like that word. It's mucky."

"Call it what you like. It doesn't matter to me, and I'm not asking out of vulgar curiosity. But I'd still like to know the answer."

She said nothing. It was good enough as far as he was concerned. He could draw his own conclusion. He said: "For how long?"

She was defeated. He got the truth. "For the last two years. Not really often, though."

He wasn't absolutely sure what she meant. He asked, "How often?"

"Only now and again. When we had to go away on conferences together."

He straightened up and eased his shoulders. He wondered how many people knew of the affair. He said, "Don't get cross with me for asking, but were there any others? Were you being, or had you been, replaced by some other woman?"

"Not that I know of." Now there was a touch of defiance. He wondered about it. Truth? Or pride?

"He enjoyed you while he still had a wife," he reminded her. "What happened once could happen often."

This time she sounded sincere. The baby mouth trembled. "I don't think so. In fact, I'm sure he wasn't like that. He was a kind man, not really a..."

16

She didn't know how to put it. He helped her. "A womanizer?"

"If you like. He was always nice and considerate but, well, you know what some men are like. I'm sure he only came to me for a change, not because he wanted me."

"A change? Who from? His wife?"

She stood up and walked slowly to the window. He stayed where he was, not knowing whether she wanted time to think, or to get away from him. There was silence for a minute or so. This told him she was trying to make up her mind how to say whatever it was she wanted him to know. At last, with her back to him, she said: "You wouldn't call an honest man a thief if he used the company's paper and envelopes for his private correspondence now and again, would you?"

"You know I wouldn't. They're usually looked on as legitimate office perks."

She turned round quickly. "That's what I was to Mr Huth. An office perk." She said more slowly: "He didn't go out and steal ... steal more paper and envelopes from somewhere else."

She sounded weary. He began to feel sorry for her. Well-disposed sorrow because by now she'd given him some help; and slightly pitying sorrow because he now saw she was far less attractive than he had at first thought. She was a different woman standing up from sitting down. Her bustline, he thought, was at least three inches too big for her height. And, for his liking, her legs in the short skirt were too thin. He envisaged her in a few years' time as a matronly pouter pigeon who would emphasize her top-heaviness by wearing vast neck furs. He felt a moment of pity for all girls with conventional but unremarkable prettiness. He felt they faded too quickly. The Krick woman had deteriorated sadly under the double blows of Huth's death and her own confession.

"Come and sit down." He said it quietly, trying to be kind. She did as she was told and drooped into the chair.

"Who found the body?"

She burst into tears and leaned forward on the typewriter. She made a miserable job of her sorrow. When he offered her his white silk handkerchief she snuffled her thanks but couldn't raise her head because she'd depressed some of the keys and the half-raised letters had tangled with her hair. Getting her free was a ticklish job which he thought he might have tried to make the most of at any ordinary time. But not now. When she looked up at him the blue eye shadow and mascara had smudged, and loose wisps of hair hung down her wet cheeks.

"You found him?"

She nodded and dabbed at her nostrils prissily.

He said, "It was a shock. Forget it. What time do you have lunch?"

"Any time between twelve and one. But I don't want anything to eat today. It would choke me."

"No it wouldn't. There's a staff restaurant, isn't there? I'll send one of my men down to get you a tray and you can eat here."

He went into the P.A.'s office and told Hill to find the canteen and fetch soup and fruit. "And while you're there," he added, "tell the manager to reserve us a table for half past one."

He sent Brant to the ground floor. "Lock all the exits except the front. Tell the constable I want to know which executives go out and when they come back."

Next he went into Huth's office. He came out carrying a glass of brandy and went back to Miss Krick. She protested, but he insisted she should drink it while

18

waiting for the tray. When Hill came back to keep an eye on her, Masters went in search of Green. So far he hadn't given much thought as to what his subordinate might have found, but Green had been away so long he thought he must have either turned up something important or drawn a complete blank and was still searching. Either way he merited a visit.

The lift filled up on its way down. He asked for the Personnel Department and was told it was on the first floor. The lift emptied at his stop, and he found himself in the middle of a steady stream of employees. He guessed they were going to the canteen. The smell of onions and fried fish hung about the corridor, mixed with the sickly smell of paper in the mass. The first door he tried was that of a stationery stock room as big as a football pitch. The Personnel general office was next to it. He went in. One girl, about seventeen, was on telephone watch while the others ate. She was dressed very much in the teenage fashion, but was as slovenly as only ill-kept, way-out garments can make a gawky girl. She was reading a magazine and eating a Mars bar out of the paper. Without looking up she said: "They've gone to dinner. Back about har' past one." She took another bite at her chocolate. He took the paper from her hands.

He said, "Where is Inspector Green?"

"How should I know? I don't know him. What d'you think you're doing with my *True Love?*"

"You'll get it back if you behave yourself. Inspector Green came down here over an hour ago to look at some records. Where is he now?"

"Oh, the cop! He's with old Torr."

"The Personnel Manager?"

"Thass right. Are you a cop, too?"

"The boss cop."

"Isn't it exciting about old Huth?"

There was no emotion in her voice: no regret at the death of her employer. Masters thought that youngsters with her choice in reading would look on sudden death as commonplace. This one found it so unremarkable as not to stir the sludge of her mind, even when it happened on her own doorstep.

He said, "Did you like Mr Huth?"

"Didn't know him." She unhooked a bit of sticky sweet from a tooth with a none-too-clean fingernail. "Never met him. Never seen him even."

"How long have you worked here?"

"Over a year now. I left my other job as soon as I'd had my holidays last summer. I couldn't stick it. In July that was. We went to Spain. Fab. Italy this year. There was a feller there..."

Masters knew he was jealous. He wanted to smack her silly face. He thought of how rarely he found time for a holiday of more than three days at once, and how few hard-working cops could ever afford to go abroad. He threw the magazine into her lap.

"Where's Mr Torr's office?"

"Just along the corridor. You can't miss it. It's got his name on the door."

Green was still with the Personnel Manager, and not liking it from the look on his face. Masters understood why. Torr insisted on shaking hands, and he was obviously the type Green had been worried about. He looked thirty-five: too old to be imitating the Americans. He was tall, with a chin running to a point as if his face had been carved from a swede. He had close-cropped hair and rimless spectacles, and he stank of He Man male cosmetics. He wore a cream shirt, harlequin tie and a suit—the colour of cold gravy—made of satin-faced drill with buttons covered in olive drab crochet.

20

The voice had a harshness, distorted by nasal resonance. Masters guessed Torr had come from within twenty miles of the centre of Birmingham.

Masters said to Green: "Found anything interesting?"

"Maybe. There's only been a few sackings. Typists come and go at a merry rate, of course, but it's of their own choice."

"We're a good firm to work for," said Torr. "I spend a lot of time and energy keeping people happy. That's how A.A. liked it. We'll miss him now he's gone."

"I'm sure you will," said Masters. "If people stay here, it must mean you treat them well. Any union trouble?"

"No unions here. In the factory. But not here at Head Office."

"In that case how do you decide on pay? Union rates, or is it decided on merit?"

"Definitely on merit. Every employee is an individual to us here in Barugt House."

Masters was getting bored. Torr was too plummy. The answers came too pat, with none of the loquacious explanations most people use for trying to qualify their answers. He thought he'd test Torr. "I'll see the records of every typist under twenty-two so I can see how you work."

"Now why should you want to do that?"

It was a tactical refusal. Masters wondered why. He decided to press the point. "Because I want to see the range of wages."

Torr leaned forward across the desk. "Now listen, Inspector, those documents are confidential."

"Chief Inspector. And there's nothing about wages that's so confidential I can't see it. I'm the soul of discretion, and so is Inspector Green."

"I'm not empowered to show them to you."

Masters felt happy. He had purposely not demanded

21

the cards, just to see how far Torr would dig his toes in. It was now clear that for some reason Torr didn't want to show them. Masters felt it was nice to know that.

"I'll inspect every sheet of paper in Barugt House if I want to. How do you retrieve data? Vibrator machine? Or computer?"

"Elliot Automation Special Selector."

"I'll trouble you to get what I want, or I'll get it myself."

Torr gave in reluctantly. He fed a heap of yellow cards into the hopper of a machine in a deep alcove. Selected cards avanced along a plastic belt towards the container. Masters put his hand down and a score piled up in his fingers. He inspected them. "Three categories," he said.

"We have to have some categorization."

"You told me you paid by merit. These categories are by age; and every girl in each category earns exactly the same wage. Are you telling me that they all have equal typing ability, timekeeping and absentee characteristics, length of service, and so on?"

"Of course not."

"Then why tell me you pay on individual merit?"

"They're only typists."

Masters put the cards down. "I'll test you. Show me the records for your salesmen."

"Medical Representatives," Torr said snappily.

These cards were blue. There were about a hundred. Masters said, "Exactly the same here. Are all these men of equal merit or are they 'only representatives'?"

"You don't understand business," said Torr. "There's got to be some categorization in a concern this size."

"I know when somebody tries to con me," said Masters. "And I like to know why. Particularly when it's over some stupid little point like this. What are you trying to do? Impress me? Or mislead me in a murder enquiry?"

Torr said: "I had nothing to do with A.A.'s death."

"Why try to bamboozle me?"

"I haven't seen A.A. for a fortnight."

"I'll believe that when I've proved it. Show me *your* record card."

"I can't. A.A. sent for it and two others a few days ago."

"What others?"

"The Company Pharmacist's and one of the advertising copywriters'. With the personal files."

"I'll know what to look for. How often did Mr Huth send for personnel details?"

"Practically never."

Masters turned to Green. "Have you seen the files of people who've been fired?"

Green said, "He says no records are kept. But now I don't know whether to believe him."

Torr started to protest. Green spoke above him. "The directors are too high an' mighty to have their details on paper like everybody else. There's no cards here for them. I reckon there must be files for them somewhere, and as our friend let slip there's a dirty great basement specially divided into cages for storing important documents, I can't see the purpose of them if it's not to store past records."

Torr said, "The chairman keeps the details of everybody who reports direct to him. And I don't know what he does with the documents when a director leaves."

"I'd still like to see your past records," said Masters. "I'll be going to the basement straight after lunch so I'll have your key now."

Torr took the key so willingly from his bunch that

23

for a moment Masters thought he'd been telling the truth. Then he remembered the duplicate and asked for it, too.

"There isn't a duplicate."

"Then there must be a master. Who keeps it?"

Masters felt pleased with himself. Torr sounded mean when he at last suggested the House Manager. Green went off to find him. Masters asked Torr, "Are you a pharmacist or a doctor?"

"No."

"Yet you're responsible for recruiting people with technical knowledge. How do you manage it?"

"I only do the advertising and prepare short-lists. Departmental directors make the final choice."

Masters stopped at the door. "I'll be seeing you again. I make a point of being interested in people who aren't absolutely frank with me. Meanwhile, just carry on with your job of keeping people happy. And don't get up to any funny business."

The directors had finished lunch and gone, so the restaurant manageress had arranged for Masters and his assistants to lunch in their dining-room. The butler, now wearing his jacket, was there to attend to them. He served Masters with gin and tonic.

Masters asked, "Do the directors drink much?"

"They're very light drinkers, sir. Usually only one drink before lunch. Occasionally a little wine with the meal, usually in hot weather. The chairman didn't like to see a lot of drinking."

"Why not?"

"He used to say alcohol in the middle of the day was not fire water but zizz water. Meaning, of course, sir, that it did not spur the gentlemen on in the afternoons, but sent them to sleep at their desks."

"Did he practise what he preached?"

"Unless he had guests, sir. Then he might take a liqueur."

"What about yesterday?"

"Mr Huth was unwell. At least, I thought he was. He came in for lunch and asked me for Tio Pepe."

"Not Bristol Milk?"

The butler was impressed. And yet, Masters thought, he must have known of Huth's private bar because it was ten to one that the chairman got his stocks—at cost—from the dining-room bar.

"Now how did you know that, sir? Mr Huth always took Bristol Milk, but yesterday he wanted something a little more astringent. He said he had accepted a cigar in his office and his mouth tasted as if he'd been smoking tram-driver's glove."

"Did he actually say that?" asked Green, standing by with a glass of Worthington in his hand.

Masters thought the question was typical of Green. A child would know that this butler could not use a phrase like that unless he were quoting verbatim.

"His exact words, Inspector. Mr Huth wasn't often humorous, although I have heard him refer to inferior cigars as 'sailor's sock.' He was always most careful, particularly when ladies were present."

"Scared of women, was he?" asked Green, gulping down the dregs of his beer.

"Shy, perhaps. When he didn't know them well."

Masters asked: "What was he like when he did know them well?"

"It seemed to depend, sir."

"On what?"

"With age he was most correct, sir. With youth he was a little more free and easy."

Green said, "You mean he liked 'em young."

The butler gave Green the look he had asked for. Masters said, "So you gave him Tio Pepe. How much?"

"He wanted to cleanse his palate, sir, so I gave him rather more than a measure."

"A port glass?"

The butler flushed. "A burgundy glass, sir. Not full, of course, but a generous measure."

"Did he have anything else?"

"Not before lunch. But I thought he began to look ill when he was at table. He just picked at his food, which was unlike him, so I persuaded him to have a brandy with his coffee."

"Another generous measure?"

"A double, sir. He really did look pale, and I thought it would do him good. I'm extremely sorry if I did wrong."

"You weren't wrong. He was ill."

"Thank you, sir. Another gin?"

Masters was tempted, but refused. He moved to the table. The restaurant manageress must have been watching through the hatch. She came in from the kitchen. When he saw her, Masters was surprised and immediately interested. This girl, he thought, would attract attention anywhere. She had the most lovely red hair he had ever seen. Not the fine hair that tends to straighten, but the coarser type that waves naturally. Although it was cut medium short there was a mass of it. He felt he would like to see it spread beside him, on a green satin pillow. Her face was round and cheerful. The sort he would have been prepared to accept as beautiful—at the right moment. Her figure was good, but plumpish rather than classical. The shape of her legs was enhanced by the height of her shoe heels: the slight chubbiness of the calves flattened and firmed by the tension on the muscles to an erotic degree not lost on Hill and Brant. They both followed her progress about the room with undisguised interest.

She stopped by Masters, close enough to make him

even more aware of her. She looked cuddly. "It's a cold meal because I wasn't sure whether you'd really be here by half past one."

"A cold meal will suit us just fine, Miss..."

"Diane Murdo."

"How long have you been here, Miss Murdo?"

"About two years." There was an unmistakable Scots brogue.

"From Edinburgh, at a guess," said Masters. "I know—Atholl Crescent."

She lifted her fine brows in amazement. "And just how would you know about that?"

"You wouldn't be the first bonny lass that's learned her art there and come down to give us Sassenachs the benefit of her training."

Miss Murdo laughed delightedly.

Masters asked: "How often did you see and speak to Mr Huth?"

"I saw him—from a distance—practically every day. As for having a crack with him, that's happened about twice since I've been here."

"Did you see him yesterday?"

"Through the hatch after he'd had lunch. He looked quite ill."

"Didn't anybody do anything for him?"

"Dr Mouncer was here."

"Who's he?"

"The Medical Director. It wasn't up to me to interfere. I only know the little bit of first aid that's included in a catering course."

"Did you ever meet Mr Huth outside the office?"

"Just once." Masters thought he detected a slight tension in her voice, and just a faint blush on her cheeks as though the question had evoked a memory that embarrassed her.

27

"Thank you, Miss Murdo. And congratulations on the lunch."

After the meal they sat alone in the dining-room. Masters said to Green, "Go through Torr's storage cage. All the signs are that there's something nasty down there."

"Any idea what?"

"Not the faintest. I've been thinking about it, and to be honest, I can't see what he can possibly have to hide."

"That's a fat lot of good. But I owe Torr something for trying to fob me off with a load of statistics about fifty-three per cent of the typists being married and a constant percentage being pregnant at any given moment. If there's anything down there I'll find it."

"Take Brant with you. Hill and I can manage upstairs."

"Are you getting anywhere?" Green made the mistake of sounding as though he hoped he would get a negative answer. Masters refused to give him that pleasure. Instead he said, "Alcohol potentiates the barbiturates."

"Like when drunks take sleeping pills and wake up dead?"

"Hill discovered Huth took brandy and sherry privately in his office yesterday. Now we've heard he had the same again down here."

"So what?"

"So we've discovered that at least he helped to kill himself."

"And we're left with only half a murder."

"Perhaps. Unless whoever killed Huth was counting on the effects of the alcohol to help the game along. If so, it was somebody close enough to him to know his habits down to the last drink. But I'd still like you to search the basement, even if Torr wasn't that close to Huth."

Sheila Krick had made extensive repairs to her make-up, and looked better for the brandy and food. She was smoking a cigarette when Masters and Hill entered the boardroom. Hill took an unobtrusive seat at the opposite end of the table. Masters sat close to the girl. She said, "I enjoyed my lunch after all. Oh! I'd better take the tray back. The kitchen staff get very angry if they're left lying about in offices."

"Sergeant Hill will take it." Hill carried the tray out to the vestibule and put it on the floor, under a radiator. When he got back Masters was telling Miss Krick he wanted to know exactly what had happened in Huth's suite the day before.

She didn't know where to start. Masters knew this was a common difficulty and let her take her time.

She said, "It was quite an ordinary day, really. Mr Huth wanted to get all the routine correspondence done before lunch because he was going to London in the afternoon for a meeting of the Association."

"Do you always call him Mr Huth to other people? Never A.A. or Admirable Adam like the other employees?"

"Oh, no. I couldn't be so familiar. He was so much older."

Masters thought her answer bore out her previous statement. Any girl who had been a man's regular mistress for two years wouldn't have been so formal. He wondered how she had addressed him on the few occasions they had been in bed together, or if she had avoided his name, making intimate moments so strained that Huth had not been eager for a more frequent relationship.

"What time was the meeting?"

"A quarter to three. It always is. But I know Mr Huth wanted to be there earlier than that because he'd written to the chairman of another company to say he'd like to meet him before the Association began."

"What for?"

"I really don't know."

"Guess."

"I can't. He often did it. Just wrote and said he'd meet people to chat about something."

"In other words he used to lobby opinion on whatever was of interest to him at a particular time?"

"I expect so."

"Did you get through the work?"

"Yes. All of it. He always kept the mornings of Association days free from interviews, and that helped."

"Who knew he did that?"

"Everybody."

"So there were no callers yesterday morning?"

"Dr Mouncer came in for coffee. He usually does every day. He stayed about twenty minutes."

"Was that when Mr Huth smoked the cigar?"

"What cigar? He always smoked them."

"Always the same sort?"

"Always. He wouldn't touch any other make."

"How did he get one he didn't like yesterday morning?"

"I didn't know he did."

"Did he leave the office at all?"

"Just once. To go to the lavatory, I think. He was only away for about two ticks."

"No other visits?"

"Not that I know of. But I went out twice to spend a penny myself, and once to see Joan Parker. She's P.A. to the Financial Director. There was one of their minutes I wanted explaining."

"How long were you away?"

"Only a minute or two each time I went to the loo, but about twenty minutes when I went to see Miss Parker. I told Mr Huth I was going, of course. I always did when I was going to be away for more than a minute or two."

"Do you think anybody could have visited him while you were away?"

"It wouldn't be likely. He never saw anybody without an appointment."

"And you're sure there was no visit arranged for about that time?"

"Not unless he made it himself, by phone, and forgot to put it in the diary. That wouldn't be like him, and I'm sure nobody in the company would ask to see him on the morning of an Association meeting day."

"Did anybody ring you up and ask you to go anywhere away from the office? To the foyer to meet somebody? Or to the pay office to sort out some mistake in your pay?"

"No. Nothing like that."

"Was Mr Huth smoking a cigar when you got back from seeing Miss Parker?"

"I can't remember exactly, but I don't think so. There might have been one on the ashtray when I poked my head round the door."

"No smell of cigar smoke? Think hard, because smells bring back memories."

She shook her head. "There always was a smell of cigars. The office has an extractor but there's always a smell. It clings to the furniture and curtains, I think."

"Did Dr Mouncer come for coffee before or after you went to see Miss Parker?"

"Just after I got back."

"And when did Mr Huth go for lunch?"

"At about twenty to one it would be. I locked his door

31

and my own and followed him out. That was the last time I saw him alive."

Masters wasn't prepared to let her brood at this point. "Did he say what he intended to do?"

"No, but I didn't expect to see him after lunch. I knew I'd be back about a quarter to two and he'd be gone by then. It takes nearly an hour to get to London by road and he wanted to be early for his meeting. When I got back his door was still locked, so as I was busy, I never went in there again. I thought he'd been and gone."

"Did he always carry his own keys?" Masters had seen them among the contents of Huth's pockets. He could see them, as Hill had laid them out, keys, cigar case, matches ... Masters paused for a moment. There was something missing. No cigar cutter. Probably he smoked the sort that didn't need cutting. He repeated: "Did he always carry his own keys?"

"Oh, yes."

"Do you always take an hour for lunch?"

"Not often. Not if Mr Huth was going to be in the office in the afternoon. But when he was going to be out like he was yesterday I used to take the full time and do my shopping. Actually I went to the launderette yesterday, so it took me a bit more than the hour, but nobody minds because I just scoot out and back again on so many days."

"And you didn't go into Mr Huth's office again until this morning?"

"No. You see, with him away, I get a chance to get away on time. So as I was a bit late getting back from lunch I rushed a bit to get finished by a quarter past five." A sudden thought struck her. She stared at him, horrified, her baby mouth open. "Do you think he might have been in there all yesterday afternoon?"

Masters said, "Perhaps. I shall have to check a bit further to make sure."

"But I might have saved him. Oh, why didn't I look in?"

"You couldn't have known, so don't get upset. What I want to know is why nobody else found him before you did this morning. Isn't the office ever cleaned?"

"Oh, it is, very carefully. But I have to be here when it's done. There was some industrial sabotage once, so Mr Huth's door was always locked when both of us were away. It wasn't cleaned by one of the outside contractors who do all the rest of the building. We have Mrs Pallot, a sort of staff charwoman, who came in at all sorts of odd times when Mr Huth wasn't here and I was."

"It sounds haphazard. Didn't she come up yesterday afternoon?"

"She has other jobs. She used to come up here at a quarter to nine when I came in, and work until about twenty past. Mr Huth got in just after that. If Mr Huth was going to be in during the afternoon she popped in at lunchtime to empty the ashtrays and collect any glasses. Then at five fifteen, if I was staying and Mr Huth had gone, she'd come in to run the Dustette over the upholstery. It was a very good arrangement really, because the office never got really dirty and it was better to have lots of regular little cleans rather than just occasional big ones. I think so, anyway."

"What does Mrs Pallot do when she's not cleaning the office?"

"All sorts of things. She's a vulgar old thing, but she fetches and carries the directors' coffee and tea trays and washes up the glass and china in their dining-room. It's always kept separate from the restaurant crockery. I think she also cleans the dining-room itself."

"Did she come up at lunchtime yesterday?"

"No, because she knew Mr Huth wouldn't be in in the afternoon."

"And at five fifteen?"

"Yes, she came. And I sent her off because I wanted to scoot myself." She looked up at him apologetically. "I do seem to have made a mess of things, don't I?"

He said, "How were you to know?" He got to his feet. "I shan't want to see you again today. If I were you I'd go home now, get to bed early, and come in all freshened up in the morning."

"I'll ask Dr Mouncer if I can go."

"You've got my permission. You won't need his."

"Thank you ever so much." She gathered her large handbag under her arm and stood up. "I do feel a bit like a lie down."

Masters and Hill went into the P.A.'s office.

Masters said: "Look into the business of that cigar. Go through the stubs in the ashtray. See if they all come from the same stable. I'm looking for an odd man out. And inspect that drug bottle, too. Inside and out. I'll be back in a few minutes."

Masters left the P.A.'s office and crossed the vestibule, leaving the lifts and the single office door on his right, the washrooms on his left. He went through the swing doors into the open plan office. He asked the first girl he saw to direct him to Miss Parker. She pointed out the door to the financial secretariat: the first on the right past the swing doors he had just come through. Inside he found Miss Parker and four other typists working under her direction.

Masters' immediate thought was that Joan Parker was the most attractive woman he'd met in years. She was really lovely: not at all the sort of girl whose good points had to be summed up before he could decide whether she was or was not worthy of attention. She was dark, tall and slim, with a figure well enough defined to rouse his heterosexual instincts the moment he saw her. He thought nobody could ever mistake her

34

for a boy, but he reckoned she was the sort Shakespeare must have had in mind when he wrote parts for girls-turned-boys. She had healthy brown skin and violet eyes. She was alive and acute. He rarely shook hands. Never if he could avoid it. But he found himself wanting to touch this woman. He made a point of holding out his hand. He sensed the soft strength of her fingers and wrist. Automatically he noticed that she was wearing no ring. He wondered how a woman so attractive had managed to fight off covetous males for so long. She grinned—definitely grinned—as though she guessed his thoughts. He felt foolish because of it. She was a teaser, he thought, but he reckoned she would play fair. He liked his own conclusion.

Masters half perched on her desk. The other girls were pretending to ignore him, but he noticed they'd stopped typing and become busy in spurious but silent activity with their copy. Joan Parker looked up at him with a grin in her eyes which showed she'd noticed the silence, too.

He said, "You've heard Mr Huth was found dead in his office this morning?"

"It's been the sole topic of conversation," said Joan Parker gravely, her eyes still making a mockery of her attitude.

"I'm interested in anybody who could have visited him yesterday morning."

"On an Association meeting day? Nobody would dare to visit A.A. on a meeting day." There was still the leg-pull in the look she gave him. He damned her eyes and looked away.

"There's no list of callers, and Miss Krick says she admitted nobody but Dr Mouncer. But Miss Krick was away from the office from time to time, so somebody could have called without her knowing. It is quite im-

35

portant that I should make sure when, and for how long, Miss Krick was absent. Some of you ought to be able to help me."

"Poor Kricky! She must be in a stew. We all feel very sorry for her, although she's not really our personality of the year. Is she so prostrate she can't give you the facts?"

He said: "Why don't you like her?"

Joan Parker didn't answer directly. She swivelled in her chair and looked at the other girls in turn, inviting them to speak.

"She's a cow," said one. "Pure Jersey," added another with a giggle. "I expect this has turned her milk sour."

"She's a bit prim, you know," said Miss Parker. "And so terribly proud of being the chairman's P.A."

Masters said, "She's given me a list of her absences. One of her visits yesterday morning was to see you."

"That's right. One of the financial minutes at the last board meeting was a bit of a porridge because my chief hadn't used a brief. Her shorthand note was verbatim, and though it was a bit muddling for anybody who didn't really understand the point being made, she should have been able to sort it out herself. But she's so afraid of making a mistake!"

Masters said, "That roughly equates to what she told me."

"I'll bet," said Miss Parker sarcastically.

"Exactly when did she come?"

Miss Parker grimaced. He thought that even when pulling a face she was attractive: as endearing as a pickle of a kid in a mess. "Now you're asking. In the middle of the morning some time, but *exactly* when..." She finished with a shrug of the shoulders and a pout which meant she could help him no further.

"It was five to ten," said a voice behind Masters. He

turned and saw a girl, wearing spectacles, who had not spoken before. She coloured under his gaze as he waited for her explanation.

"There was a tour of the Printing and Despatch Department for some of us who'd never been round it. I was just getting ready to go when Kricky came in. I had to be on the first floor at ten."

Masters nodded approvingly. "How long did she stay?"

"Don't ask me. I went out then to get a lift."

"Does anybody know?"

"I should say less than five minutes," said Miss Parker with certainty.

"Longer than that, worse luck," said the girl who had called Miss Krick a cow. "She came and yapped at me for ages after she'd seen you. You went into Mr Barraclough's office then, remember."

"Of course I did," said Miss Parker, with what Masters thought was a rather forced smile at the girl. "What a little memory-box you are, Dilly." He thought he detected a touch of annoyance in Miss Parker's voice. She turned to him.

"You see how easy it is to forget, Chief Inspector. Dilly is Miss Krick's typist. She lives in here because there isn't room in A.A.'s suite. She bashes out the non-confidential copy. There's reams of it and Miss Krick often drops in, bearing files clutched to her matronly bosom."

Masters said to Dilly, "How long did she stay with you?"

"Long enough to read through seven foolscap pages of type. She gets mad about typing mistakes, or even rubbings out, and when you're doing a report on medical things there are so many words you don't know how to spell you make mistakes because you get out of rhythm. Do you know how to spell diarrhoea? I always have to

37

look it up because I'm sure its been spelt wrong in the copy. And there's lots of other words like it."

Masters said, "Cheer up. I'd have the same difficulty. How long would you say it took her to proofread the seven pages? Fifteen minutes?"

"And the rest," said Dilly. "Don't forget she was looking for mistakes. She didn't find any but she was jolly careful."

"So if we say at least twenty minutes in all we should not be overestimating?"

"Oh, no."

"There now," said Joan Parker gaily. "We've solved part of your problem. Does it help?"

"Who knows?" said Masters, standing up.

"And if you did you wouldn't say." She walked across the room with him to the door. He thought she moved like a graceful animal. He could imagine firm, unobtrusive muscles just rippling under the brown skin. He hoped he'd have an excuse for meeting her again.

"What about the cigar?"

Hill handed Masters an envelope. "There *was* one of a different make. Only half smoked. You can see he stubbed it out. It looks like a stick of celery. I'll have it analysed."

"And the bottle?"

"It's a funny thing, but this bottle's only got Huth's prints on it."

"Has it definitely been wiped?"

"Must have been. And quite recently. The people in the factory and whoever handled it before Huth got it must have left some traces. Now there's no sign of them, and there's no blurred prints of Huth's such as you'd expect if he'd been handling it for several days."

"I half expected it. But just to make sure I'll ask the

char if she dusted it, when I see her. If she didn't, it shows that somebody definitely tampered with the bottle, and presumably with the drug it contained."

Hill said, "I don't think they did. That's the second point. This bottle's never had any pills in it. I turned it upside down and swept it out with a clean camel-hair brush. D'you know what I found?"

"What?"

"Nothing. Absolutely nothing. Bottles that hold pills get some of the substance rubbed off and deposited on the sides. This one's as clean as a new pin."

Masters took the biggest of the easy chairs, and filled his pipe. "Well," he said, "at least you've confirmed it's murder and not suicide. Look up Dr Mouncer in the internal phone book and tell him I'd like to see him, here. Now."

2

Dr Mouncer, the Medical Director, was short, thick-set and, Masters thought, aggressively well groomed. Masters put him down as in the middle forties, for though what remained of his hair was still jet black and smooth, he had quite a large bald pate. His jowls were just beginning to sag, faintly purple and suggestive of good living. He wore, like Torr, rimless spectacles, which bit deep into the bridge of his nose, giving him a hawk-like ferocity. Unlike Torr, he was dressed soberly in a navy blue chalk-stripe suit with an R.A.M.C. tie. When he came into Huths' office he had a small cigar alight in his hand. His shoes were bulled so that the toecaps gleamed like patent leather. Masters' first impression of him was that in any field he cared to make his own, Mouncer would be a force to be reckoned with. Masters supposed that as Medical Director, Mouncer would have to be a practical as well as a theoretical doctor of some standing, with a load of business acumen to help him commercially and politically.

Mouncer said, "I decided to keep my distance until *you* came to *me*. I'm in charge of the Company, of course, now that A.A.'s gone; but knowing how you work, I thought you would appreciate it if I didn't interfere." He sounded deliberately supercilious.

Masters' immediate thought was that here was a clever bastard. Mouncer had orientated that statement to make him feel beholden by using the word appreciate, and wrong by the subtle suggestion that the police should have approached him, not sent for him. Masters had met the trick before. Others had tried to influence him by verbal manœuvre before this. Mouncer, he thought, would have had a lot of practice. His position probably depended on his ability to influence doctors to use products which were, in some cases at least, no better than those of competitors. Masters decided to give no ground.

"You wouldn't have been allowed to interfere, doctor. Help, perhaps, but not interfere. I *sent* for you because I want some information. My sergeant will be recording our conversation. I suggest we sit down."

Mouncer hitched his trousers fastidiously at the knee, and then leaned back with his cigar.

Masters said, "We've found a bottle marked Nutidal. Do you know how and why Mr Huth had it?"

"Certainly. Or to be more precise, I can suggest why a Nutidal bottle could have been found here. I prescribed Nutidal for A.A. a week ago."

"Is it usual for a doctor who isn't in practice to prescribe?"

Mouncer used the handkerchief in his sleeve to polish his spectacles. He wasn't to be rushed into any reply. Masters waited.

41

"It is unusual," Mouncer said. "However, A.A. was a special case. I'd like you to understand that he had a particularly astute mind. And though he was neither doctor nor pharmacist, it follows that, for a layman, he had an extensive knowledge of medicine, disease symptoms, drug indications and the like—learned over the years spent as a senior executive in the pharmaceutical industry. So, although I was a little concerned when I visited his office last Monday morning to hear that he was ill, I was not in the least surprised to learn that he had carried out a self-diagnosis of cystitis."

"Bladder trouble?"

"A layman might call it that." Masters thought he sounded snotty and wondered whether he was being so because he was trying to hide something, or whether he was just arrogant by nature. "A medical man would call it a urinary tract infection. It's not the most difficult disease in the world to diagnose. A.A. would easily recognize that he had the classic symptoms of U.T.I.— frequency and dysuria."

"Meaning what?"

"To you? That he was urinating more often than was his custom and he was suffering pain when doing it."

"Why didn't he go to his family doctor?"

Mouncer laid his cigar carefully in an ashtray and gently flicked the front of his waistcoat before replying. Masters wondered whether the pause was being used by the doctor to decide what answer to give or just how best to put it.

He said at last, "I don't know how much you've managed to learn about A.A.'s character in the past few hours. Probably not much. So I'll tell you a few things about him. Above all, he was kind. But he was also a proud man. He would be sympathetic with anybody who was ill and, of course, his life's work was devoted to providing drugs to alleviate sickness. But he regarded any form of illness in himself as a weakness. That's point one to remember. A.A. also had a streak of pure Victorianism in him. He was very correct in company. He had a sense of humour, but it had to be clever verbal wit to interest him. A dirty story left him unmoved—even embarrassed."

"How's that?"

"He always gave me the impression that when he heard a vulgar story he thought it was being told against himself."

"Can you explain that attitude?"

"I couldn't begin to. His Victorianism worked in another way, too. I'm positive that subconsciously he would regard a urinary tract infection as the sort of disease that men like him couldn't possibly contract. He was wrong, of course, because no disease is a respecter of persons, but I'm convinced that was the reason behind his visit to me. Mention of his own waterworks to a family doctor would be taboo. So he consulted me—because *he* could tell *me* what was wrong, and so he didn't have to undergo an examination. That's point two. Do you find it hard to believe?"

Masters shook his head and said, "I met a case like this in the mass a fortnight ago."

"In the mass?"

"I was invited to present the prizes at a boys' school. It was a new building with all the latest gadgets laid on. The headmaster told me that the kids wouldn't use the showers at the end of the gym. Frightened to undress in public, he said. Same mentality as Huth, I suppose."

"Exactly. Some small children get these complexes and then grow out of them. A.A. never seemed to have done so."

Masters was trying to square this information with Miss Krick's story of occasional seduction. He couldn't manage it. He said to Mouncer, "What did you do about his complaint?"

"What any responsible medical man in my place would have done. First of all I tried to persuade him to visit his own physician, and when I saw I was getting nowhere, insisted on having a urine specimen for investigation."

"Why?"

"Because frequency and dysuria can be signs of quite a number of diseases under the group-heading of urinary tract infections. Some are mild, but they can lead to others which, if not treated properly, may in turn result in severe damage to the kidneys. You may have heard of pyelonephritis?"

Masters nodded. Mouncer was beginning to sound a bit more human now he was on medical topics. He went on, "I have a small laboratory here, so it's an easy matter to test a sample with the standard sensitivity discs. But as it take twenty-four hours to do the test fully, I immediately put him on a course of our own urinary antiseptic, Nutidal. I could have changed later if the need arose. In the event, Nutidal discs were effective against whatever pathogens were bothering him. I suspect they were common *E. coli* bugs, so I confirmed the course of Nutidal next day."

"Did you give him the drug from your own stock?"

"I don't keep a stock of any drugs. I know better than that. But I knew A.A. would want to avoid any rumour that he had the disease, so I ordered the bottle to be sent to me—where it would cause no comment—and handed it on to him myself in this office."

"How many did you give him?"

"Fifty-six. Eight a day for a week."

"Taken how?"

"Two, four times a day. After meals usually, but it's immaterial so long as the complete course is taken. As I expected, the Nutidal cleared his symptoms in a couple of days, but I insisted, as he well knew I would, that he take all fifty-six to guard against the emergence of resistant strains of the bug."

"When were they due to finish?"

"He started halfway through last Monday, so he would take four that day, eight on each of the succeeding six days, and the final four by lunchtime yesterday. I've not been told how, or even when, he died, but as he was alive at lunchtime yesterday, the bottle you found should be empty."

"I don't know when he died either. But I know he was poisoned."

Mouncer stubbed his cigar and made no comment.

Masters said, "Why weren't you called this morning when the body was discovered?"

"Because I get here half an hour after Miss Krick opens up for Mrs Pallot. By that time the police were in charge and their own surgeon was here."

"Who broke the news to you?"

"Mablethorpe. I came straight up but was told I would be contacted when I was wanted."

"Is Nutidal a dangerous drug?"

"If you mean by that does it come under the Dangerous Drugs Act, the answer is no. It's not dangerous, nor is it scheduled, otherwise I should have refused to prescribe it. It's widely prescribed by doctors, but the public wouldn't be able to buy it over the counter like aspirin. A chemist would refuse to sell it for self-medication. He'd only supply it against a prescription."

"I'd like to know more about it."

"I can assure you that A.A. wouldn't die of Nutidal

poisoning. But you'll find a binder with all our medical literature in it in the bookshelf under the phones." Mouncer got to his feet. "If you want anything more than that there's a product book which I keep. It's a comprehensive history right from the start of research into the drug, but I'm afraid a layman would find it less than illuminating."

Masters also stood up. He disliked anybody he was questioning to tower above him. He felt at a disadvantage.

"You visited Mr Huth yesterday morning?"

"For coffee at half past ten. I came in most mornings at the same time. Not for any specific reason. Merely to keep in day-to-day touch."

"Did he say how he was feeling?"

"I asked him. He said he felt all right. I thought he seemed a bit tired, and put it down to the fact that he'd been ill and hadn't bothered to take a rest to get over it."

"Did you give him a cigar?"

Mouncer raised his eyebrows. "Why should I?"

"You smoke them. He smoked them. Don't people offer their cases nowadays?"

"Not to A.A. He had his cigars hand rolled. He could afford to, of course. I buy mine by the packet. He wouldn't have looked at my brand."

"Or anybody else's?"

"Not if he could avoid it."

Masters said: "He smoked one different from his usual brand yesterday morning. We've found the butt. In addition, your butler told us that Mr Huth said at lunchtime that he'd smoked a cigar which tasted like tram-driver's glove. How does that square with what you've just told me?"

"It doesn't. All I can say is that he must have accepted a cigar from somebody whom he didn't want to offend by refusing. I *have* known him accept one from an employee whose feelings he didn't want to hurt."

"Employees smoke cigars?"

"Quite a lot of them. Ever since the cigarette and cancer scare. We encourage it, in fact. As a responsible pharmaceutical company we could take no other attitude unless we tried to ban all smoking except pipes. You can imagine what the result of that prohibition would have been."

When Mouncer had gone, Hill salvaged his cigar butt. They compared it with the remnants of the odd man out in the envelope. "No luck," said Hill. "The one we're interest in is thinner and paler than both Huth's and Mouncer's."

"Is it milder or stronger?"

"Definitely milder. I think it's a popular brand, but I'll have it checked tonight."

"Do that. It's likely to be important." Masters walked to the phone table and picked out the green binder of Barugt medical literature. Each leaflet had an earpiece with its name. He opened it at Nutidal and read for fully ten minutes. When he shut the book he sounded jovial, "Now for Green. I wonder what joy he's had."

"None if you ask me," said Hill. "Else he'd have been up here laying it on thick. Inspector Green likes to make sure he gets his share of the credit. He lets the world know when he strikes oil."

Masters said, "Don't we all?" Then the internal phone rang. He said before he picked it up, "Talk of the devil! This is probably him, now." He was wrong. It was the constable at the main entrance.

"I checked everybody out and in at lunchtime, sir. They're all back now except one. And as it's half past three it looks as if he's out for the rest of the day."

"Who is it?"

"Edward Dieppe, Company Pharmacist."

Masters paused while he tried to recall where he'd heard the Company Pharmacist mentioned earlier in the day. Then he asked, "Anything else?"

"No, sir. They all came back looking as if they'd been out for a drink and a sandwich at a pub. They do it instead of going to the canteen. There's nothing stronger than Coke there."

"Did you notice Mr Torr go out?"

"No, sir. Nobody by that name left the building."

"Thank you." As Masters put the phone down, Brant came in.

"Inspector Green's been trying to get you on the phone, but you were engaged, so he sent me up to ask you to come down to the basement."

Masters said to Hill, "Go through the files in here. Look for anything to do with Torr, the Personnel Manager, Dieppe, the Company Pharmacist, and some other chap who's in advertising. I'll be back soon."

The lift went down to the basement. They stepped out into an area of bare concrete walls and solid square pillars, subdivided into scores of tiny cubicles by chain link fencing which reached from floor to ceiling. The cubicles had frame doors with large grey padlocks. Dim light came from lowpowered bulbs in ceiling blisters. Brant led the way past doors crudely labelled with department names. Masters wondered how any business could function splintered into so many units, divisions and sections. It gave him an idea of the complexity of a modern pharmaceutical firm that owns research, development, promotion and marketing facilities.

Green was inside an open cage, using a vehicle inspection lamp fed from a power point for light.

"See this?" Green pointed to the doors of the cage he was in and the one next door to it. The open one had no label. The other was labelled "Personnel." "I'll bet he came down here at dinner-time and took off the name. Crafty bastard. You see why, don't you? Nobody else has two cages, only Torr's lot. He kept one for business and one for himself. He tried to bamboozle us all right."

"Any trouble with the keys?"

"That's what let him down. I tried the key he gave me on the cage with the name on it, and it didn't fit. I got in with the master. There's nothing in there except leaflets saying what a marvellous firm this is to work for. But I reckoned I ought to try and find out which lock the key he gave us did fit."

"And you found it next door."

"Yes. You can see where the label's been. Taken off as soon as we'd left him, I'll bet. There wasn't much else he could do unless he'd come down here with wire cutters. This fencing's tough stuff." Green picked up a sheet of paper and wiped his hands. "As soon as that key turned I knew we were onto something. And he was telling the truth when he said he doesn't keep old records down here. He doesn't."

Masters wished Green would get on with it. He'd found something, otherwise he'd have waited till the phone was not engaged, and saved Brant travelling up ten floors. Masters gestured towards the shelves in the open cage, laden with plastic bags full of papers.

"A blind," said Green. "We've been through the lot. Nothing but letters dating back to the year spit. Not worth the room they're taking up."

"I'll swear he was trying to hide something."

Green crumpled up the paper he'd been using as a towel and threw it to the ground. "He was," he said in mean triumph. "At the back there, in that cardboard box."

Masters went in. A heavy-duty, two-foot-cube carton had been emptied of bundles of industrial training pamphlets. At the bottom was a round tin, four inches in diameter and six tall, enamelled in pale green with red lettering. "Fingerprints?" he asked.

"We only touched the rim of the lid when we took it off."

Masters used his handkerchief and lifted the tin out. It was well finished, with rounded edges and a tight lid. He read the printing: "Hospital and Dispensing Pack. 1000 tabs. Metathiazanone B.P. Barugt." He set the tin down and took off the lid. Inside was a plastic bag two-thirds full of white tablets.

Masters said, "He'll say that a senior executive of a drug firm has a right to possess a large amount of one of their own products and keep it safe under lock and key."

"It'll have to be a good excuse," said Green. "He's not connected with the drug side of the firm. And he'll have to explain why he hid it down here."

"He'll have to explain that barney with the key, too," said Brant.

Masters said, "Metathiazanone sounds like powerful stuff. Do we know exactly what it is and does?" He didn't look at Green as he spoke. From sad experience he gussed Green hadn't yet disclosed all he knew. Hill had been right. Green rarely discovered anything of use, but when he did he tried to make the most of it. There was pent-up excitement in the Inspector now. Masters sensed it. Green's attitude made it appear as if he regarded the discovery of the Metathiazanone as momentous.

Green said, "It *is* powerful and it isn't."

Masters thought that if this was the way Green intended to play it, he had another guess coming. Green might be unwilling to let the cat jump before he reached what he considered to be the most impressive moment, but this time he was going to lose his opportunity. Masters deliberately switched the discussion line.

He said, "How many tablets are missing?"

"About three hundred," snapped Green. "You can see the bag's still about two-thirds full."

Masters began to back out of the cage, apparently prepared to leave the matter where it stood. Green had no choice. He now had to divulge his great news if he wanted to keep Masters' interest.

"He said, "I found these in the tin." He handed over a small bundle of certified delivery postal slips. The climax had been a damp squib. Green looked and sounded nasty. Masters looked at the slips.

Masters said peevishly, "Why the devil can't postal clerks fill these things in properly? 'Cordner E.2' isn't worth the paper it's written on as an address."

"Yes it is," said Green, a touch of triumph returning to his voice. "There's three with Cordner's moniker on them. If you'd been with us a few years back and read the bulletins you'd remember Dopey Cordner."

"I wasn't with you years ago, and I've never had anything to do with the dope squad. I suppose you're going to tell me Metathiazanone is being peddled."

"Not to humans. Dogs," said Green. "Dopey Cordner does the tracks, or rather, the kennels. I don't know exactly what Metathiazanone does."

"You said it's powerful and yet it isn't. Why did you say that if you don't know anything about the confounded drug?"

"Because I know it'll stop dogs, but I'll bet it won't kill them. And it's never been in the dope lists as dangerous to humans."

Masters accepted this. In spite of his other shortcomings, Green could be relied upon to remember facts like these. His memory was his only asset in Masters' opinion. But now Green's moment of triumph had passed. Masters took charge of the tin and asked Brant to find the Company telephone exchange. "Check up on today's outgoing calls. If they don't keep lists, grill the girls until they remember who has made calls. Go through the internal phone book, take each executive by name, and ask every girl on the board whether they've asked for outside numbers. And hurry. It's nearly knocking-off time."

Green asked, "What now?"

"There's a leaflet in Huth's office describing Meta-thiazanone. I'm going up to read it. I want you to slip out and call the Yard from an outside box. Get anything currently known about Cordner and the other names on the postal slips. Ask if Torr is known or suspected. Then join me in Huth's office."

As they waited for the lift Green said, "Are you thinking somebody fed Huth a thumping great dose of Metathiazanone?"

"That wouldn't square with your story about it not being fatal to greyhounds, would it?"

"Not unless there are some bloody awful side effects in humans."

"It's made for humans. A man ought to be able to tolerate it better than a dog. And take a lot more of it."

Masters was right. The medical pamphlet described Metathiazanone as "a gentle depressant for the central nervous system." Its action was said to be mildly tranquillizing, to relieve tension and encourage sleep. It sounded just right for slowing down dogs, thought Masters, but not for killing humans, particularly as the drug was not a hypnotic, nor was there any suggestion of phenobarbitone in the formula.

Hill was still searching through files. Masters gave him the tin for fingerprinting. Masters himself used the internal phone book to find which floor housed the Pharmacy Department. He went down to the sixth. Outside the lift was the floor plan. Pharmacy was shown as occupying about half the area: a large, open-plan space surrounded by smaller private offices. He went through the swing doors into Market Research which he had to cross to reach Pharmacy. He was conscious that all the typists were watching him closely. He was accustomed to being recognized, but this was the first time he'd encountered the grapevine workings of a big firm. He could feel the stares, but as he passed with apparent unconcern, he felt the egoistic thrill of pleasure that being the centre of attention always gave him. For effect, he stopped halfway along the room, at the desk of the prettiest girl he could see. She blushed furiously as he said, "May I?" He held out his pipe and indicated the ashtray on her desk.

"Oh, yes," she said hurriedly, and pushed the heavy glass plate towards him so clumsily that she cascaded papers onto the floor to add to her confusion. He tapped the pipe, examined it, took a paper clip from the tray on the desk, straightened the wire and dug into the dottle. When he had finished he smiled his thanks, threw the wire into the wastepaper basket, and passed on his way thinking he'd made the girl's day by giving her himself to talk about when she got home. He was still smiling with satisfaction as he went through the partition door into Pharmacy.

He could see nobody in the room but girls.

He paused and then turned to the one sitting immediately inside the door. She was looking up at him and grinning at his bewilderment. He asked, "This *is* the Pharmacy Department?"

"Too true. A folly of female pharmacists—except for the two near the window who are filing clerks. They know all about storing medical data and clinical trial reports. You're Mr Masters, aren't you?"

She sounded gay, and he thought she looked good fun. She was sitting in a swivel chair, showing a lot of shapely thigh unselfconsciously. She went on, "We have no men here, worse luck."

"Not even Mr Dieppe?"

She tutted in disgust and called across the office: "Chris, Mr Masters wants Teddy." She turned back to Masters. "Chris is our Unit Manager. Teddy's the Departmental Manager. Chris stands in for him when he's not here, which he isn't at the moment." Masters knew Dieppe was not in Barugt House, but he didn't say so.

"I'm Christine Blake," said the Unit Manager, coming over from her desk. "Vera talks too much. She'll jaw to any man." She turned to Vera. "Pull your skirt down. You'll embarrass him."

"Not likely." She stood up and tugged at the miniskirt. "It won't come down I'm happy to say. Go with Christine, Mr Masters. She's the cold, clinical, factual type. She'll tell you anything you want to know."

"Your reputation gallops ahead of you," said Miss Blake.

"And we're duly impressed," said Vera, sitting down again and showing, if anything, even more thigh. "I hope I haven't shocked you."

Christine Blake ushered him into Dieppe's office before he could reply.

"Vera who?" he asked.

"Chambers. Known as Jerry when she's being particularly difficult. She gets ragged about her name in a department like this staffed with nothing but women."

"You've a poor opinion of your sex?"

54

Christine Blake was no beauty. She had straight fair hair, glasses, a neck that seemed far too long and a flat chest. But she had an air of forthrightness and candour that made him trust her instinctively.

She said, "Individually, no. I should have thought you could have told I was a feminist, just from looking at me. It's a pastime of the not over-intelligent but definitely below-par-in-looks type of woman. I'm the only woman unit manager in the company. But unmarried women in a group...there are six of us in there, all of an age, all spinsters, nearly all pharmacists, and all earning roughly the same salary. We're too alike to make comfortable roommates. You need a cross section if you're not to get the prejudices we suffer from. We can pick each other up on the smallest mistake. And we do."

"Vera seems cheerful enough."

"She's an exception. She keeps us going. Without her there'd be a bust-up. She's the most attractive of us physically and mentally—to men, I mean—and other women sense this and, funnily enough, respect it. But don't get me wrong. In the office we're a catty lot, but outside we're looked on as being level-headed, competent, professional women. What we like is an upheaval now and again."

"Such as a murder?"

She frowned. "No. Just something lurid to gossip about. For one of us to hook one of the eligible men we all claim to know but never manage to marry. Even for one of us to have an illegitimate baby would give us something fresh to talk about."

"I sympathize," said Masters, "but I'd have thought Mr Dieppe would have leavened the lump a little."

She snorted in disgust. "Teddy? He's the biggest old woman of the lot of us."

"But clever, surely? He's the Company Pharmacist."

"Competent," she said. "No more." She sat down behind the desk and gestured to the visitor's chair. He took it. He looked about him and saw that departmental managers were entitled only to a square of carpet, not the close-fitting variety the directors had. The furniture was too modern and flimsy for him. He hadn't yet learned to like moulded plywood with all the beauty of grain submerged under liquid plastic paint.

Christine Blake went on, "Teddy's been here for donkey's years. He came from Retail because he couldn't stand the customers. In those days all the pharmacists here were men. One by one they were promoted or went to better jobs and so, through no fault of his own, Teddy found himself the senior. By then male pharmacists were not available at the salaries Barugt was willing to pay. Pharmacy is about the one profession where women really are taking over from men in a big way, so it was much easier to recruit girls."

"So Dieppe got his managership by default?"

"Entirely. He's idle. Works harder telling people what he's got to do than he does doing it. And he's got no moral courage. In a big firm like this there's cut-throat competition between departments for shares in the annual expenditure budget. We girls have to fight our own battles. Teddy won't ask for a thing in case it gets him in bad with the board. And he bows and scrapes if a director even looks at him."

"Is there no one to complain to?"

"Not in this status-ridden company. I'm being frank about Teddy—even disloyal. But he really does drive us up the wall."

"Where is he now?"

"At home with a migraine. He gets one every time there's a tricky decision to make or there's a lot of work in."

"He went off at lunchtime?"

She looked sharply at him. "If you knew, why come asking for him?"

Masters cursed himself and cast about for a facile explanation. "I know he went out at lunchtime. He might have gone home or to a restaurant for lunch and then come back again. Don't get upset at my inspired guesses."

"Detectives are pretty frightening, and murder's not funny, either."

"You know it's murder?"

"Would you be here if it wasn't?"

"It gives you the something to talk about you were craving just now."

"Not a murder among people you know. And not A.A."

"You liked Mr Huth?"

"Liked? How can you like somebody you don't know? I never saw him from one month's end to another. But we knew he was fair-minded. That's the sort of thing you can tell even in the lower ranks. A company takes its lead from the top, and when he wasn't being slightly megalomaniac, as all big bosses are at times, A.A. was an employee's dream of a boss. He didn't interfere himself, he kept slobs like Torr, our Personnel Manager, in place, and he had an eye for improving profits by improving working conditions. He had his drawbacks, but there must be much worse."

"What drawbacks?"

"He didn't get rid of Teddy and Torr and people like them who make life a misery."

"Not drink? Or women? That sort of thing?"

"If he was a drinker or had women he was very discreet about it. Not a breath of scandal reached us here, and it would have to be some secret if *we* didn't get to know about it. No, what I meant was that if you did happen to meet him he was always perfectly charming, but he gave the impression that he was paid such a vast sum every hour of the day and night that for him to spend a minute talking to one of the company's lesser lights was just pouring money down the drain. It was a peculiar trait, but he gave everybody the same feeling."

"In that case, what would be your reaction if you were told he'd called for your personal file?"

"Good lord, he didn't, did he?"

"No. A hypothetical case."

"I should be scared stiff."

"Of a fair-minded man?"

"He just didn't deal with the likes of me. I'm sure he couldn't fit the name Christine Blake to my particular face. Pay increases are done by departmental directors, so it wouldn't be anything nice like that. So it could only mean the sack."

"Didn't he ever see departmental managers?"

"Never. It's a known thing that he refused to deal with anybody except those who reported direct to him. And that meant directors only unless there was something very special he wanted to ask an expert who was not a director."

"You've given me a good picture."

"Look here, is there something funny going on with the gestapo files?"

"Gestapo?"

"That's what we call them. All sorts of people write reports on anything they like or dislike about us or our work—usually adverse, I suspect—and send them down to Torr for the files. He says it's to help with deciding on promotions and pay raises, but we think it's just a particularly nasty brand of American snooping, because we're never allowed to see what's written. You know what I mean. Over there they won't promote a man if his wife's not just so, no matter what his work's like. I'm certain it's Torr's idea and A.A. was so much out of touch he didn't know exactly what went on."

Masters felt he was beginning to understand the company. Top management could never give him a picture like this. He'd had some qualms about operating in a giant, successful firm. Now he knew that in spite of its sophisticated management techniques it was as prone to anomalies and failures in understanding as any other. He supposed it was a typical set-up, no worse than any other big concern. It succeeded in spite of its shortcomings. He turned to Christine Blake again.

"Do you make phenobarbitone?"

"In every known shape, size and form. It's a useful drug, you know, in spite of the bad reputation it's got through wrong use. We put it in all our sedatives and euphoriants because it helps in anxiety states, depression, sleeplessness and so on."

"These sedatives, they contain only small amounts of phenobarbitone?"

She nodded.

"So they're virtually harmless?"

"Harmless? Not on your flippin'. All drugs are dangerous. But if you mean are they less dangerous than the pure substance, the answer is yes, but only insofar as somebody would have to take a much bigger overdose before they killed themselves."

"What about the pure drug? Do you manufacture that, too?"

"Of course. It's useful when properly administered."

"For what states?"

"It's a sedative, an antispasmodic and a hypnotic. Small doses are sedative and antispasmodic. Larger doses are powerful hypnotic and anticonvulsant."

"And those are the only reasons for prescribing it?"

59

"Oh, no, there are other conditions where it's valuable. Epilepsy, tetanus, for spastic children and lots more, but they have to be selected individually by a doctor."

"When wouldn't it be used?"

She laughed and said, "Whenever possible. But I expect you meant to ask when would it be definitely contraindicated?"

"If that's the term meaning it definitely should not be used."

She thought for a moment. Then: "It's not as easy to answer as you might think."

"You mean I'm a layman asking the too obvious?"

"Laymen don't differentiate between side effects, toxicity and tolerance because they all seem to overlap. I'll try to sort it out for you."

He sat back and filled his pipe while she arranged her thoughts. As he struck a match she began:

"You don't often get side effects with small doses. That is, with a quarter or half a grain twice or probably three times a day—that's a maximum of six quarter-grain tablets. Larger doses, according to the reaction of the patient, can produce drowsiness, probably vertigo and nausea, headache and so on. The absolute maximum dose in twenty-four hours—not a day, please note—is ten grains, or forty quarter-grain tablets."

"More than that would kill?"

"Probably but not certainly. It depends on the timing. I think doses of up to a hundred and fifty grains have been taken and the recipient has lived. But I wouldn't advise anybody to try it unless there's a stomach pump handy. I think less than thirty grains would definitely be fatal in the great majority of cases if no treatment was given."

"Go on."

"As I was saying, the maximum therapeutic dose is ten grains, taken only under the closest medical supervision. As much as that can produce delirium, stupor, ataxia—that's incoordination of voluntary muscular movements—skin eruptions, and a score of other nasties. Those are side effects. Now conditions where phenobarbitone should never be used—that is where it is definitely contraindicated—are chiefly in debilitated patients and those with pulmonary diseases, because it makes the breathing shallow; and large doses should not be given to patients with nephritis—that's inflammation of the kidneys."

He became suddenly more interested than ever. "Nephritis? Would you have that with urinary tract infection?"

"You could have. One of the most serious of the U.T.I. is pyelonephritis which means—wait for it—inflammation of the kidney and renal pelvis. It can destroy the kidneys if it isn't cleared up, or if it's exacerbated."

He thought she had the right word. He wondered if Huth's kidneys had been inflamed with his infection, and if the drug which killed him had exacerbated his complaint in his last few hours. He said, "It's all very interesting, and I'm sure you're an expert, but the number of tablets you mentioned seems very high to me. Forty!"

She smiled and ran her fingers through her hair. It was so straight and simply dressed that the upset made not a ha'porth of difference to her appearance. She said: "It's very difficult explaining everything at once. I didn't want to confuse you by telling you there were different sizes of tablet. I've stuck to the smallest, which weigh fifteen milligrams, with a quarter of a grain of phenobarb in them. There are half-grain and one-grain tablets, weighing thirty and sixty milligrams each. A who wanted to give a larger dose would use larger tablets, and correspondingly fewer of them. Does that answer your question?"

"Perfectly. What size are the tablets?"

"The quarter-grain size is minute. Like those little tablets of saccharin you sweeten tea with. Wait here a moment and I'll show you some."

Masters stood just inside the door and watched unobtrusively as she went to her desk, collected a bunch of keys from the centre drawer, and then opened a grey metal cupboard which he saw was packed with bottles of drugs. She stood for a moment, locating what she wanted, and then took three bottles from a shelf. He was back in his seat before she turned round.

He examined the different sizes of tablets and then asked, "Are they small for their weight?"

"Very. They're hard compressed, and though I don't know what the excipient is—that's the inert material the tablets are made of—it must be very dense. I could show you quite a few other tablets which weigh the same but are much bigger."

As she poured the tablets back he said, "They're Dangerous Drugs? Under the Act?"

"Schedule 4.A. To supply them a chemist needs a doctor's signature, but not the patient's."

"Who signed for these?"

"Oh, lord," she groaned. "Teddy, as Company Pharmacist is responsible for all the legal requirements of the Drug Acts. Don't tell me you've spotted something wrong with his system, otherwise he'll be away with migraine for a month."

"Is the cupboard in your office really secure? It looks to me like a tin box I could open with a bent paper clip."

"So you watched! I might have known it. It's your job, of course. And you're right about the cupboard, but what are we to do? We have to have sample supplies in this department. If we were to ask for something more secure it would mean a capital requisition for a safe. Teddy would rather die than ask for it, and even if he did, they'd fob him off and refuse to fork out. They'd make us store somewhere else and we'd be chasing up and down stairs all day. We're very careful, you know."

"Are you? Who uses the key, other than yourself?"

"All the pharmacists."

"You keep the keys in your desk drawer?"

"Always."

"Overnight?"

"Yes."

"Is the office locked?"

"Good heavens, no. The cleaners have to come in."

"Is your desk locked?"

"Usually. There have been times..."

"When you've forgotten or gone off early? I know. What about lunchtime? Do you all go together?"

"All the girls. Teddy minds the shop until we get back."

"And he's in here working with the door shut, while anybody can come and go unnoticed in your office where you've left your drawer open so that he can get the keys if he wants them."

"That's about the size of it," she confessed. "This office is a right of way to the back stairs and so many people pass through we never even notice them."

"What sort of a check do you keep on your private stocks?"

"None. But it could be done. There'll be a signed request from a doctor for every scheduled pill sent out. You'd have to check back through the letter files to find it, though."

Masters stood up. "I'd rather you didn't say too much

of what we've talked about. You know I'm interested in phenobarbitone, but I may be mistaken, and I don't want to start rumours."

"I'll stall the girls somehow, but they'll be like a pack of hungry wolves."

"It's nearly a quarter past five. Hometime for you. Why not dash off and avoid awkward questions?"

She stood up and said with a grin, "If you'd invite me over to see the Black Museum I really would have something to tell them."

He said, "I'm not letting you add my scalp to those others. But I'll see you again."

He'd remembered Mrs Pallot.

She didn't often get the chance to go home with the office staff at five fifteen, but because she wasn't allowed to clean Huth's office she had her hat and coat on ready to go when Masters found her in the cleaners' locker-room on the ground floor.

He didn't like the look of her. She was ugly and overdressed. He thought she must have bought her coat and hat for best some years before and had now replaced them with another set. She might have looked in place in chapel on a Sunday night with an eye veil dotted in sequins, but not in Barugt House. Her lower lip protruded and showed a line of whitish pink flesh that looked unhealthy.

"Mrs Pallot?" he asked.

"That's me." The voice was hoarse and she showed the tip of her tongue as she spoke. "What d'you want?"

"I'm Chief Inspector Masters."

"I thought you was a copper. You pick your time, don't you? I'm off home so don't be long-winded."

"Miss Krick told me about your arrangement for cleaning Mr Huth's office, so I won't ask about that.

64

But I should like to know if you dusted a brown medicine bottle on the desk yesterday morning."

"There wasn't no bottle—leastways not a medicine bottle. Plenty of booze in the cupboards."

"You knew he kept drink there?"

"Seeing there was empty glasses to wash most days I'd be daft if I didn't."

"How many glasses?"

"Just one or two. Until this week, that is. Then there's been three or four a day. He'd probably taken to drink, and no wonder with that Miss Krick always about. She's as fussy as her backside that one."

"Would you say Mr Huth was a big drinker?"

"Big? Not him. Not nearly so big as my old man, but he took a drop more than most knew. Not that it mattered if he did. He was a nice feller. A real gentleman."

"I've heard he took very little."

She grinned knowingly. Her teeth were badly stained. "That's because he was clever. He didn't want the others to drink overmuch in the directors' dining-room. So he pretended to have just one in there. But he could have a private nip when he felt like it. None of the others kept any in their offices."

"You were with Miss Krick when she found him?"

She buttoned up her collar and flung her head. "Was I, indeed? She was with me, you mean. Getting hysterics all over the place."

"Who told the police?"

"I did. I could see he hadn't died natural. I've seen too many dead 'uns not to know. Dialled 999, I did."

"You've got your head screwed on."

"It's commonsense. Now if you've heard all you came for I'll get home and get my old man's tea."

He let her go. She brushed past him in the doorway, banging his shins with her full shopping bag. He watched her paddle away out of sight and then walked to the lifts. The other three were waiting in Huth's office.

Green said, "They'll let me have a report on Dopey Cordner tonight. The boys were pleased with the news." Masters knew Green would have laid it on thick at the Yard about how he had discovered the Metathiazanone and the postal slips. He decided he didn't give a damn. It might result in the dope squad taking Green off his back.

"I was lucky," said Brant. "They keep a tally of all outside calls except those to the factory. That's a permanent open line, so they don't keep count. Torr made five calls."

"Who to?"

"I don't know yet. I've only got the numbers. I'll have them checked overnight. It's bloody funny really, because they didn't use to book calls, but Torr made them start. Now he's perhaps going to get the chop because of it."

Masters said, "Did you find anything, Hill? You did? Can it wait until morning? The building's nearly empty now, so we shan't see much more of the staff today. I'm going to Huth's house in Richmond. I'll go home by tube."

"Do you want me with you?" asked Green.

"No. It'd be bad for your blood pressure. Big house. No egalitarianism. Besides, there's still one more job here for you to do before you go. Get hold of the night security man who should be coming on now, and ask him if Huth's car was here last night when he came on, and if it was here all night."

"What sort of a car is it?"

"How the devil do I know? It shouldn't be beyond your powers to find out."

Green grew angry. "And what the hell does it matter

if it was here? Huth was here. That's all we want to know."

"I want to know if Huth was in his office all yesterday afternoon, dying."

"That'll help, I suppose?"

"It might." Masters turned to Hill. "Ring up the secretary of the Association—the number's bound to be in the book somewhere—and ask him whether Huth attended yesterday's meeting. And don't be put off by a simple 'no.' Make sure he was expected to be there, just in case he told people here he was going but wasn't really intending to."

"What if he's left his office?"

"Chase him at home. Give me the answer in the morning."

The house was even bigger than Masters had thought it would be. In the darkness it loomed, unlit, before him. He thought Huth must have splurged after his earning power had soared.

There was no sign of servants. Mrs Huth answered his ring and let him in after he'd told her who he was. She appeared to be alone in the house. He guessed she was slightly older than her husband: in her middle forties. She was tall and big-boned, with iron-grey hair cut straight with a fringe. She was wearing a tweed skirt and fawn cardigan, and one leg was swathed in an elastic bandage under the stocking. She wore low-heeled shoes and walked with a slight limp. He thought she looked competent: just the sort of woman to mother fine sons, but who might easily be a failure with daughters. She was emphatically not his idea of the wife of a youthful industrialist, and as far as he could tell she showed no signs of distress at her husband's death.

He liked the house but not the furnishings. There were none of the economies of the born well-to-do. No loose covers to make a still serviceable suite last a few years longer. No old piece pressed into use in a modern setting because it would have been wasteful to throw it out. The furniture was expensive, but had not been collected over the years. He imagined he could have ordered it all in one day from the various departments of any one of the big stores. The patterns of carpets and curtains were futuristic. The lampshades were cylindrical and hung at uneven heights. The upholstery reminded him of battledress serge.

She showed him into her sitting-room. He felt it impersonal and couldn't reconcile it with the impression he had of the woman.

He said, "Who told you your husband was dead?"

"Superintendent Bale. He rang at a quarter past nine this morning. Soon afterwards, Dr Mouncer rang, too."

"I must apologize for not getting in touch with you myself before now."

"You must have been very busy." Her voice was clear, with none of the despondency he would have expected.

He approved her attitude. It made it easier for him, and he admired courage. "I shall have to ask you some questions. Personal questions. Probably painful ones."

She said, "I once read that in any case of sudden death the police investigate the next of kin very closely."

She'd had all day to prepare for a visit. He wondered if she'd rehearsed her part, it was so well controlled.

"Mr Huth was murdered."

"I hadn't been told, but I guessed as much. The Superintendent was very guarded when he spoke to me."

"And Dr Mouncer?"

"Not very sure what had happened. When you arrived my suspicions were confirmed. You deal almost exclusively with murder, don't you?"

"Murders are the only cases that get into the papers.

I've plenty of less lurid ones to deal with in the average day's work. However, I thought I might have met you earlier."

"You're surprised I didn't call at Barugt House?"

"Yes."

"I was obeying orders. I asked the Superintendent if I should go over and he said he would prefer me not to. Perhaps he thought I should be hysterical. Dick Mouncer also suggested I should keep clear and let you come to me when you wanted to see me. So you see, it wasn't sheer indifference that kept me away; and, of course, I went to the mortuary this afternoon."

He felt she was rebuking him, as though he had suggested she had neglected her wifely duty. It often happened. People read more into simple questions than a mere request for information. He regretted this woman had done it. She seemed to be too perceptive to make such a mistake.

He said, "I didn't mean to imply you were indifferent, and I'm sure you were being co-operative, but I thought you would have been anxious because your husband didn't come home last night. Weren't you surprised that he didn't?"

"Not particularly. He said he might stay in London."

"Might stay? Not definitely?"

"Adam was not thoughtless about letting me know his definite movements. He always did whenever possible, but for the past five or six years he's been difficult to keep track of. These American firms are restless, you know. Opportunists. They expect their top men to dart about, finding new openings for markets, creating trends favourable to their own marketing techniques, pressurizing competitors, and finding new ways of doing everything under the sun in the hope that some graph will plateau higher up the scale or run off the chart altogether."

"Did he stay away very often without letting you know he definitely wouldn't be home?"

"Not often. But often enough for it to be no cause for surprise. He kept an overnight bag ready packed in his office in case he had to go off somewhere at short notice."

"Without picking up the phone to let you know?"

She hesitated a moment. Then: "I was out sometimes when he rang."

"No servant to take a message? Couldn't his P.A. have rung you when you got home?"

"I've said that his unexplained absences were very occasional, and usually he'd warned me to expect them."

"When they happened were you worried?"

"Not after the first few times. I didn't like it, of course. No woman would."

He asked, "What did you think he was doing on these occasions?"

"Work." There was no compromise in the answer.

"Did he always tell you afterwards where he'd been and why?"

"Yes. Always." The shortness of the reply was defensive, he thought. Why was she not enlarging on the circumstances which had kept Huth from home without warning?

He said, "Thank you. You can see I had to know if he was expected home last night or not. And if he was, why no enquiries had been made as to his whereabouts." He realized he was talking like a constable in the witness box.

Although he had put no question she said, "We are— were—a sophisticated couple. We were often apart during our married lives. Adam was a sales manager before he went to Barugt as Sales Director. In both jobs he found it necessary to be away for days at a time, trav-

70

elling round his field force, going to lectures, meetings, and medical symposiums. Since he became chairman he has travelled even further afield, to Europe and America, as well as in this country. We never clung in the sense that we couldn't be apart."

"Now you'll be alone altogether?"

"I have two children. Both away at school."

"And you'll be all right for money?"

She didn't claim her affairs were no business of his, but explained the position quite readily. "Adam had a current salary of fifteen thousand a year. That sounds a lot—it is a lot—particularly before tax is taken off. But you must remember he only had that much for the last two years. Six years ago, when he became chairman, he had ten thousand. Before that we had between two and four thousand." She gestured round the room. "All this cost a lot of money which we could well afford if the salary had continued. Now the situation may be different."

"Will there be a pension?"

"No. Unfortunately the Barugt scheme only allows a man to decide whether he will take his own full pension, or take half and leave half for his wife should she live the longer, during his last five years in the company. Adam was only in his forties. He would have had to wait until he reached sixty before making the choice."

"Insurance?"

"There I shall be lucky. The company pays a lump sum of three times the annual salary for death while still employed. And, of course, there are private policies, too."

He said, "So apart from your husband's estate, you will get over fifty thousand pounds."

"I shall invest most of it for the children and then go back to teaching."

"You are a qualified teacher?"

"I taught in a girls' grammar school. I have a degree in chemistry."

He said, trying to sound as if it was of no importance: "And although you might have grown a bit rusty at teaching, you've kept your science up to date with pharmaceuticals?"

"You could say that. I made no conscious effort to learn anything of Adam's work, but the knowledge has accumulated almost unnoticed, through conversations and reading journals."

"Do you know a bit about every side of the business? Things like advertising and packaging, for instance?"

"Packaging, certainly. I was always being asked whether I would prefer to buy pills in bottles, bubble packs, or tear-off strips; whether I thought pale pink was a suitable colour for pediatric product wrappings; and whether I thought slide boxes more convenient than foam-lined pouches for carrying soft pills in a handbag. I found it very interesting."

"Did your husband ever bring samples home?"

"Goodness, yes. Our family medicine chest is full of them. Just those it's safe to use for self-medication, of course."

"No scheduled drugs at all?"

"Not one. I wouldn't have them in the house because of the children, and we've stuck to that rule even though the children are growing up and are away from home now."

"What about some non-scheduled drug like ... well, say Nutidal, which is one of the big sellers, I believe?"

"We wouldn't have that, would we? It's a specific. No use for any illness except cystitis or some other urinary infection."

Masters watched her closely. "Your husband was taking Nutidal at the time of his death."

72

"Adam was?" He could have sworn the surprise was genuine. "He never told me. Who prescribed them for him?"

"Dr Mouncer."

"Why didn't Adam tell me?"

"Dr Mouncer said he was reticent about such things as urinary tract infections."

"He was, I'm afraid. He was brought up in a very Victorian household, and both his parents were getting on a bit when he was born. One didn't mention certain things. A lot of that attitude could still be found in Adam."

"If his attitude was so strait-laced, would you say that he was unlikely to have had any women friends? Other than yourself, I mean."

"I don't quite understand what you mean by women friends. Wives of friends and acquaintances? Or do you mean had he a mistress?"

"A mistress."

"Who knows?" For the first time he thought he could detect a note of bitterness in her voice. "Perhaps he had, without my being aware of it. It would be in keeping, wouldn't it? Wasn't the Victorian paterfamilias supposed to have been the biggest rake of all time?"

"That sounds as if you have had your suspicions."

"Nothing of the sort." She rose and limped over to a side table. "Can I get you a drink. I should have offered you one when you arrived."

"I'd like a gin and tonic, please."

"I didn't expect you to say yes."

"Why not?"

"Policemen on duty just don't—or so we're led to believe."

"A popular fallacy." He walked across to collect the drink. "I'm on duty twenty-four hours a day. If my superiors want to call me out at three in the morning,

73

cancel my leave without notice, or send me to Timbuc-
too, they can do so and I've got no grounds for complaint.
If I never drank on duty I'd never have a drink."

She walked back to her chair with a glass of brandy
and ginger. He followed and sat down again. She didn't
touch her drink. She said, "I can see where your questions are leading."

"I warned you they might be painful."

"Do you realize that nobody has yet told me how
Adam died? I've seen his body, so I know he wasn't shot
or coshed. So I imagine you're not looking for a thug.
If he was poisoned—and I think he was—you could be
looking for literally any type of murderer. Including a
partially crippled, but otherwise healthy, woman who
is now a widow with a motive worth fifty thousand
pounds. At this moment you are obviously trying to
credit her with a desire to be rid of a husband who was
deceiving her." He held up his hand to stop her. She
went on: "No. Please let me finish. What I can say in
all honesty is that I was not aware that Adam was
having an affair. And one other thing: I did not leave
the house last night, though I realize that in a case of
poisoning whether I left home or not could be immaterial."

"You said you had no knowledge of an affair. Did you
have any suspicions? On the nights he didn't come
home?"

"I don't believe I did."

"You're not sure?"

"You don't want suspicions or opinions, do you? Aren't
you interested only in facts?"

"Hard facts are just the kernel of the nut. What sur-
rounds them has to be cracked."

"So you'll believe just what you want to. Or have you
proof that Adam was carrying on with some other

woman? Have I really been blind? The last to know?"

"I shall believe what you've told me. Until I've reason not to."

"You haven't answered my question."

"I'm not here to answer questions, but I'll explain my thoughts. If I find a man staying away from home at night without giving his wife an explanation before he goes, I immediately suspect another woman. And I'm usually right. So I've questioned you on this point, and I shall go on probing until I know for certain that there isn't another woman involved. It sounds dirty, but my job, and murder, are like that. But it doesn't mean that I automatically disbelieve everything I'm told. I've said I believe you."

"But the suspicion that I killed my husband still remains."

"It's got to. I know that whoever murdered Mr Huth was somebody very close to him. So I can't exclude anybody in that category—least of all you—until I know the answer."

"He *was* poisoned?"

He nodded.

"That's why you were so interested in my knowledge of pharmaceuticals." She picked up her glass, and with the first sign of nervousness she had shown, held it to her lips with both hands and drained it. She put it down and looked at him. "But why all those questions about packaging?"

He didn't reply. He put down his empty glass and stood up. She rose and stood beside him. "Thank you at least for saying you believe me about Adam, and for being so frank about the situation I'm in."

She showed him out. He walked away wondering whether people like him were not sometimes very lax in confirming facts. He'd believed Miss Krick's admis-

75

sion that she had been Huth's mistress simply because it seemed unlikely that any girl would say she was involved if she wasn't. But what if Krick had been yearning for her employer's favours and had dreamed up the seductions she claimed had taken place? He felt this exempted him from guilt for the half-lie he had told Mrs Huth. He had no *absolute* proof of her husband's unfaithfulness.

By the time he caught the tube he decided he was only having this debate with himself because he liked Mrs Huth. And that, he thought, was not a good thing at the moment. He had to stay impartial.

3

Wednesday morning was again bright and fair. Though they set out in the early part of the rush hour, Hill made good time because the main flow of traffic was inwards to London. Masters told Green of his talk with Mrs Huth. Green annoyed him by saying, "She sounds a fly customer. Ramming her own motives down your throat like that."

"I don't think so," said Masters. "It would have been useless for her to try and hide them. We'd have found out soon enough."

"That's what I mean. She knew she couldn't keep it a secret how much money she'll get, so she blurted it out to show you how truthful she is. But you notice she didn't admit anything she thought you couldn't prove. She didn't say she knew her old man was carrying on with another woman."

"I thought she was telling the truth."

Green replied with a curl of his lip. "Garn tittle! Any

woman knows whether her old man's having a bit on the side or not. You get married and see."

"Krick says it didn't happen often. It could have escaped Mrs Huth's notice."

"Blow that for a game of soldiers," said Green offensively. "I'll bet what Huth sampled once he'd want again pretty often. Probably not with Krick because she's a bit prissy. I tried to have a parley-voo with her yesterday and all she could say was 'Pardon? Pardon?' to everything I said. She struck me as the sort who'd be frightened of getting her hands dirty in bed."

"What about the common belief that the wife is always the last to know?"

"Did she pull that one on you, too? Well, of course, she would. I'd believe it if the wife was some downtrodden little dumb cluck without a word to say for herself, but you say Mrs Huth is pretty wide awake. She's got enough *nous* to know what was going on, and to tell you she didn't know. It's an old trick. First she tried to defend herself by telling the truth, then when she saw she'd got you round to believing her she started the lies. What I'd like to know is why she did it. If she's got nothing to hide."

Masters remembered his own half-lie of the night before, and said: "Everybody's got something to hide. It's not easy for a proud woman to admit her husband preferred somebody else."

"Not easy. But it's safer, in a murder case. She'd be able to work that out all right. So why not say so?"

Masters grudgingly admitted that there was some logic behind Green's argument. But it was all based on supposition. He decided to ignore it, and said no more until they reached Barugt House. Green had the keys to Huth's suite. He opened up. The rooms were stuffy from overheating and too much stale smoke.

Masters sat down in one of Huth's armchairs. "We're early. Nobody'll start work here for another quarter of an hour, so we'll get up to date among ourselves. What about Torr's calls?"

Brant took a list from his pocket. "He made five calls yesterday, all to the addresses on the postal slips."

"No others?"

"Not by Torr. There were over a hundred outside calls altogether. They've all been checked. Four to wholesale chemists. Twenty-eight to retail chemists. Six to hospitals. Seventeen to doctors. One each to the Telegraph information bureau, a sound studio, an industrial photographer, a printing firm, and then a lot of private calls to all sorts of places—electricity showrooms, house agents, people's own homes and so on. I don't think there's anything to interest us except Torr's calls."

Masters said: "Good. That'll save us a lot of bother." He turned to Green. "Did the Yard have anything to say about those contacts of Torr's?"

"They phoned me at eleven last night," grumbled Green. "They took their time about it."

Masters was irritated at the reply. He hoped Green had been in bed and had been obliged to get out to answer the phone. He asked, "What did they say?"

"They liked it. They've known for the last three months that somebody's been stopping dogs. There's been a rash of it all over the country, but they've not got on to who's doing it because whoever it is has been boxing clever. They've never nobbled a favourite."

"What the devil have they been doing then?"

"Stopping second and third favourites."

"To make sure the favourites won?"

"That's the idea. It hasn't always come off, but the chances of them winning have risen so much that a system of betting on favourites only would have more

79

than paid off. And it's made it a good thing for place betting on unnobbled outsiders at long odds."

Masters said, "Somebody was willing to take smaller but surer pickings over a long period rather than make just a few big killings before they were rumbled?"

"You're learning. There's somebody with a little bit of brain behind this. Clever enough to see that little bits and pieces add up to a hell of a lot in time. And that's not Dopey Cordner, nor anybody like him. They'd rush in for the easy money and give the game away in no time."

"But Cordner is implicated."

"There's no proof yet. But he's been getting about a bit more than usual these last few months. It took some time for the penny to drop with the course authorities. They don't normally think there's been any hanky-panky if the favourite wins, because the odds laid on favourites are small, and made smaller by any bets laid at the last minute, after the doping's been done. Mobs don't usually go to so much trouble for small returns. That's why they've been getting away with it for so long."

"Does the squad know the drug that's being used?"

Green grinned in triumph. "Metathiazanone! I told you they were pleased. They hadn't been able to trace the source, but they were on to what I told them like a sparrow on a crumb. They'll sew it up now for sure."

"Who were the others Torr was in contact with besides Cordner?"

"Chaps I've never heard of. But they're known. A Pole called Janowski, a scrob Norwegian called Gudbjartssen, and a couple of cockneys, Symonds and Blair."

"Any of them likely to figure as the brains of the outfit?"

"The squad says not. So Torr may be our boy, and if Huth had found out about him..."

80

Masters interrupted: "Don't let's jump to conclusions."

Green said, "Hell, he's a prime suspect."

"According to you, so was Mrs Huth a moment ago."

Hill said hurriedly: "I found the three files you told me to look for. Torr's, Dieppe's and Hunt's."

"Anything in them?"

"There's nothing we want actually in the files, but there were some notes about all three of them on Huth's desk diary for last Wednesday."

"Show me."

Hill brought over a loose-leaf, page-a-day diary on a wooden stand. He handed it to Masters. The messages were cryptic: "Hunt—sf starter. Gd ad orientation. Ideas. See? Promote." "Dieppe—lacks responsibility. M coward. Pr Admin. Keep???" "Torr—missing ret products. Tape. Con Man???"

Green looked over Masters' shoulder and jabbed a stubby finger at the note about Torr. "See? Huth was on to him. Called him a con man. He'd found out about those Metathiazanone tablets and knew Torr had got them. How much would they be worth?"

Masters said to Brant, "Give me that green medical folder from under the phones. We'll find out the cost."

The literature gave the basic N.H.S. cost of a week's treatment at three tablets a day as five and sixpence. Masters worked it out roughly and said, "A thousand tablets are worth just over thirteen pounds."

"Not much," said Green. "But still the boss was on to him for having fiddled thirteen quids' worth of stock, and was likely to ask awkward questions which were not only going to stop the racetrack game, but finish Torr's cushy job as well. What about that? No boss keeps a chap he thinks is a con man."

Masters made no reply. Damn Green's eyes! There

was something in what he'd said, but it was too easy. Masters knew it and didn't know what to say to shoot it down effectively.

Fortunately Brant stepped in. He said, "Did Huth actually see Dieppe? Look at what's written. If that's what the boss actually thought about him I reckon he was going to be given the sack. Don't forget he's a chemist, so he'd know how to poison somebody. And if he really was a moral coward he might be the sort that's easily panicked into murder."

Masters said, "So now we've got three suspects. Mrs Huth with a motive and a grievance, Torr discovered at his doping game, and Dieppe niggled at getting the sack. Anything else? Oh, yes. Huth's car. What about that?"

"It was here all night," said Green. "They use Janus security men, and the one that's doing the early stint this week says they check the car park at six and again at midnight. Huth had a Daimler two-and-a-half-litre V8. It's parked under cover. There's an open-fronted space for half a dozen directors' wagons under the first floor. The Janus man found the Daimler at six. He was surprised because he'd already been round the building and knew Huth's suite was locked and in darkness. So he felt the engine. It was stone cold. He thought it must have broken down and Huth had left it for repairs."

Masters said, "Lucky he felt the engine. It confirms Huth didn't take it out in the afternoon and come back here later."

"And he didn't fetch up at his meeting," said Hill. "He ought to have done. He was supposed to chair it. The secretary said he didn't ring through here and ask for Huth because he thought he was probably held up in traffic and would arrive soon after the meeting had started."

82

"Right," said Masters. "He was here all afternoon." He turned to Green. "Take Brant with you and trace the tin of Metathiazanone back to the start of its journey from the factory. Find out how Torr could have got hold of it."

Green relished the thought of putting Torr through the hoop. He went off rubbing his hands. Masters asked Hill to see if Miss Krick had arrived. Two minutes later he was sitting facing her. She looked more composed. The black suit she wore contrasted so strongly with her milk and roses complexion and her unnaturally pale hair that at first he thought she was wearing less make-up. He soon saw he was wrong. She had even more on.

"How are you this morning?"

"Quite well, really, all things considered. Better than I thought I would be."

"That's what early bed does for you. Ready to answer some questions?"

Miss Krick settled herself in anticipation by wriggling her bottom into a more comfortable position and then holding her hands together in her lap to show she was ready. It reminded him of a matron of fifty or a child of five. The thought came to him that Krick was a mixture of the two. She looked up at him as if begging him not to be too severe, although, paradoxically, giving him the feeling that she might enjoy it if he were to be.

He said, "How often did Mr Huth go to Association meetings?"

"At least once a fortnight. They weren't all full meetings, though. He was on some of the committees."

"Was the procedure in the office always the same on those days as it was the day before yesterday?"

"Oh, yes. We had quite a strict little routine for meeting days."

83

"He always left about half past one?"

"Well, perhaps not always, but I can't remember a time when he didn't."

"He never went up earlier and had lunch in London?"

"Not since that entertainment law came in about three years ago. Anyhow, it was before I came. The Company won't pay for lunches which can be got just as easily here. That's why the dining-room has been made so nice: so that directors can entertain people here just as well as in a restaurant in London."

"Did you always take a full lunch-hour on meeting days?"

"Yes." She giggled. "I like to seize my opportunities."

He couldn't see the joke. He said, "And when you got back Mr Huth had always gone?"

"Not always. Mostly."

"How did you know if he had or not?"

"If he was still here, his door would be unlocked and I'd look in."

"Did you always try the door?"

"Every time I went into my room I tried it. If he was in I told him I'd arrived. If he was out but expected to come back I unlocked the door ready for him. If he wasn't coming in, I just tested the door and left it locked."

Masters said, "This is very important, so I must get it right. You say if he wasn't due back you always left the door locked?"

"Oh, yes, definitely. I told you it had to be locked if Mr Huth and I were both out of the office. If I'd opened it up when I knew he wasn't coming in I'd have had to lock it every time I went to powder my nose. I always left it locked so that I shouldn't forget it. It was easier not to make a mistake like that."

He thought it seemed reasonable. She was the sort who would work out little safety routines for herself, and Joan Parker had said she was frightened of making a mistake. Whoever had poisoned Huth had counted on Krick not going into her employer's office once the door had been locked and he was supposedly away.

"Now for something else," he said. "When I first saw you yesterday you were typing from a tape. Was it one of Mr Huth's?"

"He'd left several for me to do. I thought I'd better get on with them. I hope I didn't do wrong? They were in my office. I didn't take them from his."

"You were quite right to do them."

She smiled with relief. Her large bosom seemed to deflate slightly. "Oh, I'm so glad I haven't been a nuisance."

"Did any part of what you'd typed—yesterday or earlier—deal with some returned supplies that had gone missing, or have anything to do with personal files and personnel matters?"

"No. But I'd only got to the middle of the first one when you came in. There are three still to do."

"I want you to help Sergeant Hill listen to them all in a minute or two. Can you turn your Grundig to loud so that you can both hear?"

"Yes."

"One more thing before I go. Yesterday, when I asked you how many P.A.s there were, you said status changes occur with monotonous regularity. What did you mean by that? I've heard this word status since then. It seems to be important in Barugt."

The question puzzled her. She looked towards Hill as if for help, but he remained wooden-faced. At last she replied: "I meant exactly what I said."

"Expand it. Tell me what you mean by status. How does it work, or affect work? Anything you can say about it."

"Well, this Company is awfully status-conscious. We actually have little books printed with everybody's name and status in it. Directors have letters after their names and we others have numbers." She giggled again. "I'm 007. All the P.A.s are. We're the lowest grade of senior staff. Senior officers are 006. Then come all the managers in order." She counted on her fingers. "Unit are 005, departmental 004, district 003, area 002, controller 001. It's really too silly to be funny."

"Anything else?"

"Oh, yes. Status decides whether you'll work in an open-plan office, share an office, have an office to yourself, have a carpet, a coatstand, a bit bigger carpet and a wardrobe, or wall-to-wall carpet and your own choice of decoration. It really is silly because the system doesn't work for lots of reasons."

"Why? If, as you say, the Company is so status-conscious?"

"Well, all us P.A.s are 007's, which means we should work in open-plan offices, but we get offices to ourselves like departmental managers. That sort of thing goes on all the time. Even some little typists are put into private offices to keep the noise down, while their principals work in open-plan areas."

"I've seen it myself," he said. "Christine Blake is the only woman manager, and they haven't even managed to give her a cubby-hole of her own. But what about the status changes you mentioned?"

"With us, you mean? The P.A.s?"

"Yes. Use yourselves as an example."

"If you earn under a thousand a year, you're not on the senior staff list. None of the typists and secretaries get as much as a thousand, except the P.A.s. It's nice to get on the list because, besides getting the pay, you get little privileges like not signing in and out each day.

When girls first come, they're usually taken on as typists, even though they can do shorthand and filing as well. After a bit they can become secretaries because girls are always leaving to get married and have babies. That means the typists go up in status on the junior staff list. If they stay long enough, and are good enough, they might be appointed as P.A.s to directors, and then they get the lowest form of senior staff status. Daft, isn't it?"

He asked, "You followed this route yourself?"

"Oh, no. I came here as a fully trained P.A. for Mr Huth. He had to advertise when his previous one left because there was nobody he fancied for the job at the time. All the others worked their way up."

"I've only met one other P.A. Miss Parker. Wasn't she here at the time?"

"Yes, but she'd just become Mr Barraclough's P.A., and Mr Huth couldn't snitch her away."

"Tell me her story to illustrate how the system works."

"It's simple, really. She was a typist in the Pharmacy department first, I think, but I'm not absolutely sure because it was before I came. Then I think she was secretary to the controller of Research and Development. After that she became P.A. to Mr Barraclough, the Financial Director."

"And that's typical of all the P.A.s?"

"Except me."

He got up and said, "Thank you. Now would you let Sergeant Hill hear the tapes?"

He left as Miss Krick started fussily to instruct the already knowledgeable Hill in the ways of tape recorders. He went into Huth's office and looked up Hunt in the internal directory. The copywriter worked in Publicity on the fifth floor. Masters decided to walk down the back stairs. On the way from the stairs to the working area on the fifth he passed the door of the library, and outside it, in the passage, the Company museum. He paused to glance at the exhibits. Nothing more than examples of all the packs of every drug Barugt had ever marketed. Nothing but a glass display case of limited interest, he thought as he moved away.

The Publicity Department was plainly important in the life of Barugt. It occupied most of the fifth floor. Both sides were lined with offices with small pens for typists outside each one. The girls were queuing at the morning coffee trolley, each taking two cups. One for her boss and one for herself. They were too interested in choosing buns from the trays to notice him as he slipped past, glancing at the labels on the doors. He saw "Dark Room," "Studio," "Administration and Traffic," "Publicity Director," "Publicity Medical Adviser," "Scheme Manager," and then three copywriters' offices. Hunt's was the first of these.

As soon as he went in, Masters sensed an air of normality he had found nowhere else in the building. Hunt was short and podgy, but still young and bouncy rather than leaden. His eyes twinkled behind round lenses, his mousey hair stood up in a coxcomb. His full cheeks were ruddy with health, and he smiled easily, genuinely and cheekily. He was in his shirt sleeves, grey slacks, and a pair of rubber-soled pigskin shoes that needed a brush. He danced silently round from behind the desk, where he was drawing stick men on an artist's block, and held out his hand.

"I know who *you* are," he said gaily. "Earn yourself an honest penny, Chief Inspector. Come and be photographed in the studio. For an ad. Headline: "Whenever I search for the best remedy for any ailment, I find it at Barugt Products.' It'd make the best testimonial ad I could possibly get for our non-ethicals."

Masters said, "I'll take your offer up when I retire. But that won't be for twenty-five years yet. Right now I want a chat with you."

Hunt gathered a heap of various coloured job bags from his visitor's chair. "I'm always ready to forget mailings, dropouts, earpieces and what have you. Sit down. The trolley's outside, so I'll get you some coffee before we start."

When they were settled, Hunt sat back and lit a small cigar. He said, "I'm dead keen on knowing how I'm supposed to be connected—however remotely—with A.A.'s sudden departure."

Masters said, "You're not—I hope."

"Courtesy visit?"

"Hardly. I try not to waste my own time, even if I'm not so particular about other people's."

"Blunt, but honest," said Hunt. He sat back and blew smoke into the air where it hung in a flat-based cloud a foot above his head. Masters sauntered over to the window and opened it. Then he began to fill his pipe.

Hunt said, "Sorry. We're hothouse plants here. I take it you haven't called to discuss the mystique of copy-writing?"

"I might touch on it. But to begin with, how well did you know Mr Huth?"

"I *didn't* know him. I hardly ever saw him unless I happened to be visiting the tenth and wanted a widdle. He and I used to meet in the stalls, as it were, more often than anywhere else."

"Did he talk?"

"Banalities mostly. He complimented me once or twice on ads he knew I'd done. Nothing more. I never attended a conference or had an interview with him."

"What did you think of him?"

Hunt interlaced his fingers behind his head and leaned

back, elbows wide, showing the damp sweat marks in the armpits of his shirt. He rolled the cigar in his lips, and without taking it out, said, "Hard to say. I think on the whole I liked him. As much as one can like a bastard who's so remote he's harder to get at than the moon. A.A. fancied himself as an adman, you know. Lots of manging directors do. It's funny how everybody can write better copy than those employed to do it. They never think they'd make a better rep than the chap on the territory, or a better research chemist than the one already in the lab. But ads!" He sat up and leaned across the desk so that the edge made a deep cut across his bulging stomach. "All they think about is impact. Show a picture of a beauty queen in a bath, bending over to look for the soap, and you get immediate impact. But it won't sell medicines. Not one reader in a million would be able to tear his eyes away from the picture to look at the product name."

"Is that what Mr Huth wanted you to do?"

"Oddly enough, he didn't. Give the devil his due, he took a great deal of care to analyse our work. He could see what we're trying to do because, strange as it may seem, we don't just play it off the cuff. We work to a marketing plan. A.A. criticized from time to time, but by and large he was as fair-minded as you could hope for in any boss who thinks he could do your job better himself."

"If Mr Huth had no direct personal contact with his staff, didn't you find communications inside the Company difficult?"

"The ivory tower complex always does make difficulties. But, at least, with A.A. you did know you could never get near him even if you went after him with a fighting patrol, so you didn't waste time eating your heart out for a chance to have your say."

"Somebody got near him. He was murdered."

"I don't know how they did it. As far as the likes of me were concerned he was inaccessible. If he took an interest in his senior staff he never showed it openly."

Masters tapped out his pipe. "What do you suppose the reaction of an employee would be if he knew that Mr Huth had called for his personal file?"

"If it was me, I should reach for my hat. A.A. wouldn't show interest in any but a director's file unless there was something mighty serious afoot. And anything mighty serious means the boot in this Company."

"People are often fired?"

"Not often. But there have been a few sudden disappearances among the upper crust from time to time. Nobody has ever heard whether they've gone of their own free will, or whether the old dodge of giving them three months to find another job has been pulled. I think the latter, mostly."

"Three months sounds like generous notice."

Hunt said soberly, "For a man who has made a porridge, perhaps. But it's not quite so generous if you've pulled your weight, worked your way up, and then disagreed with the chairman over some small point. When you've got to get one in a hurry, senior jobs just don't seem to be there."

Masters said, "Mr Huth called for your personal file a week ago."

"Did he? Now I know why you're here. Oh, lord, what's gone wrong now? To the best of my knowledge I haven't put up a black unless..."

"Unless what?"

"I'd been doing a bit of thinking about our methods of approach to doctors—in ads, of course—and I came up with a few very revolutionary ideas. Like a fool I put them on paper and gave them to the Publicity Director. A.A. probably got hold of them and decided that they—and I—were useless."

"You didn't hear from him?"

"Not a dicky bird. I wonder where I stand now?"

"Stop worrying. I've seen a note he made. He approved of your ideas."

Hunt sat back and grinned. "You wouldn't be fooling a chap?"

"Despite appearances, this is a serious investigation."

"Maybe, but I wouldn't put it past your lot to lie like Ananias if you thought it might help you."

Masters didn't reply. He frowned, still remembering the half-lie he'd told Mrs Huth. Hunt misconstrued what he saw. "Sorry," he said. "You must be on the up and up. If it were the other way round, I'd have been out on my ear by now."

Masters silently thanked Hunt's particular brand of logic and said, "Are you absolutely sure that if Mr Huth was not satisfied with an employee he would react very quickly?"

"As sure as I am of anything. If A.A. thought a chap unsuitable, one word to his hatchet man, Torr, would ensure the execution took place there and then. Sentence first, verdict afterwards. Torr is descended from a long line of unusually common hangmen. I know a few who have disappeared inside an hour, with a month's salary in lieu, and with cards and superannuation settlement to be sent on by post, later."

Masters was thinking this didn't square with the image he had of Huth, but Hunt appeared to be telling the truth, at least as far as he could see it. He had just come to the conclusion that Hunt was probably confusing the actions of Huth with those of Torr when the copywriter bounced up out of his chair and asked quickly, "Here, you weren't thinking that because A.A. had asked for my file I murdered him, were you?"

"Not yet."

"Thank the lord for that. But it's what you came for, isn't it?"

"To look you over. And for other things. We try to be very thorough, and I personally find that a bit of friendliness often pays off. When people realize I'm not too much of an old bastard they chat me up."

"And give themselves away. I know. What were the other things you came for?"

"Do you make a cure for migraine?"

Hunt stared in surprise. "By jove, you go off on some funny tacks. A cure for migraine? Hardly. If we could find a cure we'd all be able to retire next week. What we have is a treatment for migraine which in a lot of cases eases the pain and cuts it short. Sometimes it even stops an attack, if the sufferer is lucky. It's an ergotamine preparation, no better and no worse than half a dozen others on the market, generally speaking, but it suits some patients better than anything else. That's the point with drugs that are alike. They all have their adherents, so you can't stop making any of them."

"But I suppose your job is to make doctors think yours is the best?"

"That's putting it crudely."

"What about the employees in Barugt House who suffer from migraine? Do they use it?"

"I shouldn't think so. A prophet is not without honour, etcetera, and it's well known that everybody who suffers from migraine has his own favourite method of dealing with it. So have doctors. Injections, analgesics, ergotamines, darkened rooms...you pays your money and you takes your choice."

"Do you suffer from it?"

"No, thank you. But there must be at least a dozen who do. *And* they're proud of it."

Masters said, "Now who's lying?"

Hunt leaned forward earnestly. "It's true. I assure you it is. Listen. A week or two ago we started a special campaign to push Vasocon—that's our product—and as we'd not mentioned it to doctors for a couple of years, we decided the reps should have a brush-up course on it before they went out to talk about it. We take these things quite seriously here, and reps are trained pretty carefully, not only in our own products, but in all-round medicine. The course opened with a general lecture on migraine, given by a hospital consultant—a top man. Now when we start a campaign like this we coordinate all our forms of promotion to make sure everybody's got the party line and tells the same story as appears in the ads. So for this lecture we invited everybody who gets in touch with doctors—Publicity, Field Force, Pharmacy, Marketing, Research, Trials and lots of other odd bods who creep out of the woodwork at times like this—to attend. It was a jolly good lecture, professional and unbiased. Not in our favour just because we were paying the piper. Anyhow, after it was over people were hanging about in the training room, drinking coffee, and one thing stood out a mile. All the migraine sufferers had got together in a bunch to compare symptoms and their own particular forms of treatment. They were actually bumming their chats about how often they got attacks, what the first signs were, when it was most likely to happen and so on. They went at it twenty to the dozen, trying to outdo each other with lurid details. The rest of us looked on flabbergasted."

Masters said, "Most people enjoy talking about their operations, but that's not to say they enjoy undergoing butchery."

Hunt spread his hands. "Exactly the view I'd have taken before that meeting. But I was so curious I got hold of the consultant and asked him to listen in. You know what he did? He laughed—at my surprise—and then told me that migraine is nothing more than a defence mechanism in people who can't accept responsibility. He said it's a well-known medical fact that if you can persuade a migraine sufferer to swop to a less exacting job the attacks often diminish, or stop altogether. He recommends it to his own patients and lots of those who have accepted are grateful for the advice."

"Is that everything he said?"

"No. He was on his hobby-horse, and went on for some time. Whittling it down to basics, he said that migraine sufferers use their attacks to curry sympathy. They can pass jobs on to soft-hearted people who are always willing to help out somebody in trouble."

"He meant that without the escape provided by migraine they would be unable to cope with a demanding world?"

"That's it exactly. But all sufferers aren't using it as an escape. There are some really genuine cases. Some even get migraine in the stomach."

Masters said, "Pull the other one. It's got bells on."

"It's true. I can show you references in medical textbooks if you've got the time."

"I'll take your word for it. Was Mr Huth at the lecture?"

"No. But I should think he gave the lecturer lunch."

"Dr Mouncer? Mr Dieppe? Miss Blake? Miss Chambers?"

"All there." He thought for a second. "You've met Vera Chambers, have you? Not bad, is she? I'm interested in that quarter myself, but I'm a bit doubtful. Some say she's a bit too full of fun, if you know what I mean."

Masters said, "I don't know much about her, but I got the impression that she's just *clean* good fun. You'll always get some people misinterpreting people like Miss Chambers. It's usually wishful thinking or failure. So follow your own instincts, and you won't go far wrong." He got to his feet. "Thank you, Mr Hunt. I've enjoyed the chat."

"So've I. Any time you want the lowdown on anything or anybody in Barugt, get in touch. I'm always at the same address. And thanks for the advice. It sounds good."

While Masters had been talking to Hunt, Green and Brant had been occupied in tracing the history of the tin of Metathiazanone. When he left Masters, Green had been thinking of nothing but getting even with Torr. Before he reached the lifts he began to wonder how on earth he was to set about the job.

"Where are we going?" asked Brant.

"Don't rush me. I'll have to think this out."

Brant said, "We can't go straight to Torr himself, that's for sure. He'd say he knew nothing about it; and because of that master key we can't prove he put it there."

"What about dabs on the tin?"

"Plenty, but whose are they? We haven't got Torr's yet, and you know the Chief won't let us take anybody's prints without he gives the word first. I could get them easy enough—on the sly—but what good would it be? The Chief would rumble it if we made use of them, and you know how dead nuts he is on everything being done as he says."

"You're as bad as he is. Just because a defence counsel shot him to bits for taking dabs on the sly once before!"

"He says it opens up pitfalls in court."

"Pitfalls my fat aunt!"

"So you want me to get Torr's prints?"

"Forget it. Hasn't this wigwam got a general office?"

Brant said, "So far we've only been interested in specialist departments in this place, but there must be a central office to do the ordinary chores of the Company."

Green pushed the lift button. "We'll ask Mablethorpe. Commissionaires know everything, and I've taken rather a shine to this one."

"I know. I saw you grin when he didn't knuckle under to the Chief yesterday. Me, I thought the Chief was good not to lose his temper. V.I.P. lifts! What the hell next?"

"Watch your step," growled Green.

The lift stopped at the ground floor. Mablethorpe took off his glasses and put down the racing paper he was reading.

"General office? We don't have one by that name, but there's a big department called Business Services on the seventh. It deals with reps and sends out samples and has a typing pool. It does all the odd jobs that crop up."

"That's what I want. Who's the boss?"

"Ask for Mr. Reculver. He's the manager. He's been with the Company a long time. His office is a glass one, at the end of the floor away from the lifts, so's he can keep an eye on all the girls he's got working for him."

Mablethorpe was right. Reculver *had* been a long time with the Company and he let Green and Brant know it as soon as they found him. For several minutes he deplored modern youth, modern management techniques, the shortcomings of every department but his own, and topped it all off with a list of jobs which were not rightly his to do, but which were, nevertheless, shunted onto him.

While Reculver talked, Green summed him up as being almost sixty. He was a large man, tall and fat, with a full head of white wavy hair and already, so early in the day, a white stubble. Green thought he must use an electric shaver when he really needed a razor to carry him through the day. In other respects, however, Reculver was well turned out. He wore a plain green tie with a grey-green two-piece, well pressed, but with trousers slightly too wide for current fashion because the taper from so wide a waist would have been too much for a tailor to cut without achieving the effect of a pyramid standing on its apex. His semi-stiff white cuffs were spotless and his loose collar had short points held by a plain gold pin.

Green explained their presence. "I've been told that if we want to know anything about this Company we should come to you."

Reculver puffed his cheeks. "Quite right. I deal with everybody, and everybody deals with me. I've been everything in Barugt from technical representative—in the days when we really were representatives—up to my present job which they had to give me because they knew there was nobody else who had such an overall knowledge of the Company."

Green suffered in silence. He knew people who talk too much always say more than they mean to. He comforted himself with this useful thought. At last he was able to interrupt. "What I want you to do is to tell me about the drugs people can get hold of in Barugt House."

Reculver waved his arms. "Drugs? There are hundreds of packs all over the place. I've pleaded with them to tighten things up, but they either take no notice or do something so ineffectual it makes little difference. My samples are all kept strictly under lock and key, I promise you."

Reculver was another cigar smoker. Green had expected him to be. His type always followed the lead of the big boss. He offered them round and gave them lights from a chromium table lighter in the shape of a polar bear eighteen inches high. The desk was cluttered with such objets d'art. Green was fascinated by a pair of spherical glass paper-weights enclosing pictures made from coloured sands. An elaborate glass and silver inkstand, a rotating ashtray, a twelve-sided desk tidy in moroccan leather and a turn-on perpetual calendar completed the collection. Green thought Reculver was playing at being the complete businessman, or that he might have a family completely devoid of imagination when it came to buying Christmas presents. To Green it was highly suspect.

He said: "Suppose you or somebody else about your level in management wanted a large amount of one of your drugs for his own use, how would he go about getting it?"

Reculver blew out his cheeks. "Go to the Company shop. It's on the first floor and opens at lunchtime every day. You can get ordinary packs free, but a large amount—that's different. What do you mean by a large amount?"

Green didn't tell him. Instead he asked, "Are the drugs you give away dangerous?"

Reculver was at his most pompous. "All drugs are dangerous. You can only get the simple family remedies at the shop."

"What about the real drugs?"

"Definitely not available."

"So what would you do if you wanted some of them?"

"I never have, so I haven't thought about it. You'd have to resort to what is known as a fiddle. But as fiddling seems to be a common pastime these days, I've no doubt it can be, and is, done. Not from my store, of course. I take good care of that."

"I'm pleased to hear it. Where could they be fiddled from?"

Reculver straightened the bric-à-brac on his desk as

though reluctant to answer. But he finally came out with the answer without further asking. "The P.O.D., of course."

"What and where is that?"

"The Pharmaceutical Order Department. On the fourth floor. It's part of the Financial Services Division. Archie's Pitt's the manager. Not that he'll agree anybody could fiddle anything from him, but I know—although some others don't, or won't, realize it—that if he makes one mistake a day in his orders he makes thirty. He's frightened to take a grip, you see. And that's where you'll find a loophole, mark my words."

"Pitt is inefficient?"

Reculver didn't deign to reply. He grimaced in disgust. Green was thankful. He and Brant were able to hurry away before Reculver started another lecture on the shortcomings of everybody in Barugt House with the exception of his own department.

The P.O.D. had no private office. Its members occupied a corner of the main financial floor. The place was overcrowded and noisy. Typewriters, adding machines and other equipment filled the tightly packed desks. Green and Brant had to pick their way past the backs of employees whose chairs almost touched the desks behind them. Archie Pitt sat with three women clerks, a battery of telephones, order pads in a variety of colours, and heaps of ledgers. The women were using the phones to take customers' orders, answer complaints and trace the whereabouts of deliveries. They made hieroglyphics on complicated forms and plonked them into trays to be sent to the despatch and pricing units. Pitt, tall, thin, and lugubrious, was dealing with the written orders. Before him was a pile of envelopes still to be opened; beside him, those he had already dealt with. When Green and Brant finally managed to reach him and indicate—rather than say—that they wanted to speak with him, he grew visibly uneasy.

"You're the police, aren't you?" he shouted. "What do you want to speak to me for?"

Green recognized he had a compulsive panicker to deal with. He despised them; despised anybody who wouldn't stick up belligerently for their rights. Besides, Pitt reminded him of the lay preacher who used to visit the chapel Green had been forced into attending twice every Sunday when he was a boy. The lay preacher had preached long and unintelligible addresses. Green had hated him with all the loathing bored youth could muster. And yet, to his surprise, as soon as he had paralleled Pitt with this preacher, Green felt some compassion. The touch of memory softened him. Many people were dismayed by a police visit, he thought. Not because they'd anything to hide, but because, subconsciously, they felt that if the police approached them, they must be guilty of some misdemeanour. Uncharacteristically, he tried to reassure Pitt. "I'm not here to question you personally. Only because you're manager of P.O.D. I want some general information about supplies."

The noise in the office was too great for anybody to hear clearly. Green noticed that everybody using a phone kept a hand over the ear away from the handset. But Pitt must have become attuned to the hubbub. At any rate he seemed to have understood what Green said, and he relaxed slightly.

"Can't we find somewhere a bit quieter?"

Pitt got up and led them to a small, glass-partitioned office. He explained that the regular occupant was taking the last week of his holiday and wouldn't mind if they used his office for a few minutes.

Green took the seat behind the desk and asked Pitt to sit opposite him. As there wasn't a third chair, Brant stood by the door. When Pitt saw him there, he half rose. Green felt a surge of revulsion at the thought of a grown man becoming panic-stricken at being cut off from his colleagues in the free world of a hell-hole office.

Green said, "I want to know how, if I wanted them, I could get hold of some drugs for myself."

Pitt stammered: "What exactly is it you want, Mr... er...?"

"Inspector Green. I don't actually want anything. This is hypothetical."

"Oh, I see. Well, in that case, there are several sources of supply. Mr. Reculver keeps all the professional samples in his store, to fulfil representatives' offers to doctors. Of course, not all the packs he keeps are sample packs. Quite often we use the smallest counter packs as samples, particularly when a product has been on the market a long time and we're no longer sending out assessment supplies on a wide scale. You could get some of those. Then there's the Pharmaceutical Department. They deal with direct requests from doctors for specific products for specific cases, and send them off with all the information about the drug. They might be willing to help you if the circumstances warranted it. Then there's the Publicity Department who from time to time will have a large supply of some particular drug they're promoting. You will find them only too pleased to get anything they may have left over off their hands. Then there's the Company shop which supplies medical products free, within reason, and sells things like toothpaste, soap and cosmetics at reduced prices. That's all, I think."

Green asked bluntly, "What about your set-up?"

"The P.O.D? Dear me, no. Not really. I deal with customers' *orders*. I very rarely handle stock itself."

"But you do sometimes?"

Pitt frowned with worry. "Very infrequently, Inspector."

"Who does the packing up of orders, then?"

"Why, the despatch department at our factory in Birmingham, of course. We do the paper-work here, and send a courier's bag of orders up to them each day."

"That's the laid-down drill, is it? You never change the routine for any reason at all?"

"For very urgent cases I phone an order through so that it can be dealt with immediately, instead of taking its place in the queue."

"But if some local hospital near here wanted some drugs urgently, would you still have to send to Birmingham for them? Wouldn't that be a waste of time? Some poor sinner might die while you were doing your paper-work."

"In a case like that, one or other of our sources of supply here in Barugt House would be able to step into the breach."

Green said, "So what you're telling me is that you never have drugs in your possession?"

Pitt glanced round at Brant, standing between him and the door. Green realized he would have liked to escape. It was as good as an admission that Pitt was worried. Green decided to press. He said: "Come on, man, I want the truth. First you said you did sometimes handle drugs, now you're trying to say you don't. Which is it?"

Pitt looked at him like a rabbit at a stoat and said, "Well, you see, all our stationery has the address of Barugt House printed on it."

"So what? It's your head office, isn't it?"

"Yes, yes. But you see, if customers wish to complain, they always write here, even though it's a mistake by the factory they're complaining of."

"What sort of mistakes does the factory usually make?"

"Despatching goods."

"You mean they send out the wrong drugs? That's typical. You shove up a damn great notice saying you're all working in the cause of humanity, and then you don't bother to let doctors and chemists have what they ask for first time. No wonder the Health Service doesn't pay its way."

"Not wrong drugs," said Pitt, getting excited. "You've got it wrong. It's wrong amounts of the right drugs, usually."

Green said, "Oh? And what does that mean, exactly?"

"It's very simple really. We have various pack sizes of all our products. Small ones for over-the-counter sales, and big ones from which chemists dispense their prescriptions. If a chemist orders twelve bottles each of a hundred tablets and he receives a hundred bottles each of twelve tablets, he's got the right amount of the correct drug, but not in the packs he asked for. So, because smaller packs are dearer than bulk, he gets cross and complains."

"I should think so."

"And though it's the despatch people's fault at the factory, the complaints always come to me. As if I'd done wrong. It's grossly unfair. I've pointed it out time and time again but nothing is ever done about it."

Green said, "I know what it's like to carry the can for something you haven't done. But are you sure your own department never makes mistakes?"

"Sometimes," Pitt conceded reluctantly. "But it's not our fault. It's very difficult to hear properly through all that noise in the main office. And you know what the telephones are like these days. Every line seems to be a bad one. And some pharmacists don't really seem to know what they want when they ring up and they forget what they've said after they've said it."

"Why don't you get your union to investigate?" asked

Green. "You can't work under bad conditions. It could be dangerous, with drugs."

Pitt said stiffly, "We don't have unions at Barugt."

"More's the pity. Go on. What happens when chemists receive the wrong orders?"

"That's just what I've been telling you. They send them back. Not to the factory. Oh, no. To me. Just because this address is on the invoice."

"So that's how you occasionally come to handle drugs. What happens then? Do you send them back to the factory?"

"Yes, we do. And a fine business it is, too. The work it involves! Old invoices to be cancelled, credit notes raised, new orders, new invoices. It really is appalling."

"Too bad. I suppose you keep a file of all the mistakes the factory makes?"

"I certainly do," said Pitt with feeling. Then he faltered. "You don't want to see it, do you?"

Green nodded. "Get it now." He winked at Brant and smirked with satisfaction. Brant went with Pitt to fetch the file.

It was a simple story. The letters in the file showed that a hospital pack of one thousand tables of Metathiazanone, sent out in error for smaller packs, had been returned by the customer to Pitt, had then been sent by Pitt to the factory, but had never reached its destination. Disclaimers and accusations had been exchanged, but the pack still remained unfound. The factory, in its final memo, had insisted on charging the cost of goods to the P.O.D. budget, and to make sure its views were known, had sent copies to a management distribution list which included Huth.

Green saw there had been many cases of mistakes in despatch, but in every instance—except that of the Metathiazanone—the returned goods had reached the factory safely. He said to Pitt, "How do you think this Metathiazanone went missing?"

Pitt was nervous. "I really can't be expected to explain its loss, Inspector. I return goods to the factory, if needs be, twice a week on the lorry which runs to and from the factory every Tuesday and Friday. They are stacked in the loading bay on the ground floor to await collection with everything else that has to go."

"They're what?" asked Green.

Pitt said plaintively: "It's obvious that I can't store them in my office area. My assistants carry them down as soon as we get them. After that they make out the return-goods note and send it to the factory with the mail. What happens after that is none of my business. All I know is that the tin of Metathiazanone went down to the bay. The factory say they never received it." He sniffed. "As like as not they lost it themselves and then accused us to cover up their own carelessness."

"You're wrong there. I've found it."

"You have? Where? Why didn't you tell me before? This has looked very bad for me—my department. And I've worried about it. I'll send one of my assistants to collect it from you."

"Not yet, you won't," said Green. "I still want it. But don't worry about the thirteen pounds. It won't come off your pay now it's been accounted for."

Pitt seemed happier when they left him. He shook them by the hand at the door. Green remembered the lay preacher who had looked so much like Pitt had always made a point of shaking hands with every member of his congregations at the chapel door. He hoped he wouldn't have to interview Pitt again. Nostalgia and dislike didn't mix well in Green. It made him unsettled.

"It's clear what happened," said Brant. "Torr nicked it from the loading bay."

Green said, "Strikes me anybody could nick enough dope to knock off half the Smoke if they'd a mind to. Press that lift button and let's go and tell his nibs what he wants to know."

After leaving Hunt, Masters had gone in search of Dieppe. Vera Chambers grinned amicably as he entered Pharmacy. "Teddy's in. That is, he's in the building, but not in his office. He's been running about like a wet hen all morning."

"Migraine gone?"

"Conveniently."

Christine Blake came over. "Good morning, Chief Inspector. I should wait a minute, if you can spare the time. Teddy'll pop in again in a moment. Since he heard you'd been looking for him yesterday he hasn't known whether to stay or go. What a man he would be in a crisis!"

"Yes, stay and talk," urged Vera. "Christine hogged you all to herself yesterday afternoon and then was so mysterious about it we're all intrigued."

"I'll stay to see Mr Dieppe."

"Poor Teddy!" said Vera. "He is in a stew. I can just imagine him having to make up an urgent prescription. All fingers and thumbs. Thank heaven for women pharmacists."

"Is it a good job for women?"

"Must be. There's more of them every day. It's one area where we women really have broken in."

"When they're broken in, do they like the work?"

"Mostly. But a lot find Saturday work a bore," said Christine Blake.

Vera said impishly, "It has its moments. Particularly when men are too frightened to ask for what they want when they see a girl behind the counter. We sell millions of razor blades that way."

Christine said, "Darling Vera boasts that she rarely lets them go without what they came in for."

Before Masters could reply Dieppe hurried in with an armful of papers. The Company Pharmacist differed from the mental picture Masters had built up of him. Dieppe was in his middle forties but still had the looks of a handsome youth, with unblemished skin that gave the impression of being too soft for a man who shaved daily. His hair was fine and so pale gold it shone white in the artificial light. The lips were full, red and moist; the eyes nervous and quick. He was a short man, but well proportioned and nimble on his feet, which never appeared to be entirely still even when he was halted. The way he jiffled his legs reminded Masters of a child who wanted the lavatory urgently.

Christine said, "Teddy, this is Detective Chief Inspector Masters."

Dieppe said quickly, "I really haven't time to see you now. I'm exceedingly busy."

"I think we'd better get our interview over," said Masters quietly. "Now. In your office."

"You really can't expect to upset our routine like this. This afternoon would be much better."

"You could have started another migraine before then," said Masters.

Dieppe was outraged. "Well, really!"

Christine said quietly, "Go on, Teddy. Mr Masters doesn't bite. He's rather sweet, actually."

"Oh, very well." Dieppe's eyes darted round the office, then he pirouetted on the spot and hurried off towards his own room. Masters followed slowly, and closed the door behind him.

"Sit down, Mr Dieppe," he said firmly. "I'm not here to make trouble for anybody who hasn't bought it. What I want is to finish the case as quickly as possible, so that we can stop interfering with people's work." He thought Dieppe had not taken in a word of what he'd said. The impression was strengthened when Dieppe opened a drawer in his desk and then shut it again without looking inside.

He said: "Of course. I understand. I'm an investigator, too, you know. I investigate drug properties." He laughed unexpectedly, as though he had cracked a good joke: but it was a short, tinny laugh that had little humour in it. Masters thought it did nothing but emphasize that Dieppe was in a highly nervous state, and he wondered why.

"Good," said Masters soothingly. "We shall be on common ground." He offered his pouch across the desk. "Do you smoke a pipe?"

"No. I tried it once. I can't get on with a pipe."

Masters thought that Dieppe was the least likely of men to take to staid pipe-smoking. He was probably a wet smoker: the type that would drown a good bowl of Warlock Flake. Dieppe helped himself to a cigarette, and started to smoke it in quick little puffs. Masters waited a few moments to let him simmer down, but noted that in so short a time the end of the cigarette between the lips grew moist and dark. It was Dieppe who broke the silence. His nerves wouldn't let him be quiet.

"I've been looking in here on and off all morning in case you wanted to see me."

"It's your office. Why leave it at all?"

"I've been busy elsewhere."

"Then why did you try to put me off just now?"

"Oh! Things crop up, you know. Urgent things that can't wait. The Company Pharmacist's at everybody's beck and call. I provide a service, you see."

"I'll try not to keep you too long. Miss Blake gave me most of the information I wanted yesterday."

Dieppe glanced quickly round the room and murmured more to himself than Masters, "I hope she gave you the right answers."

"She did. I'd say she was a responsible girl." Then he added, in the hope that it would help Dieppe: "She reflects great credit on your training."

Dieppe was pleased. "She's coming on. Not very good on paper yet." His mood changed. He grumbled: "She can't take any work off my shoulders on the writing side yet." He spoke for two or three minutes of the difficult technical nature of his job, and of the difficulty in finding a pharmacist capable of assisting him. Masters thought that Dieppe must revel in having people believe he was overworked. A weak man's attempt to give himself importance in the eyes of others. Masters let him stumble on, disjointedly, as he picked up files and papers to illustrate the points he was trying to make, and put them down again, unexplained.

When Dieppe finally paused Masters asked, "How often did you speak to Mr Huth?"

Dieppe said shrilly, "Never."

"You must have seen him occasionally."

"Once in a blue moon. He was ... I hardly ever spoke to him."

"When was the last time?"

Dieppe became even more flustered. He stubbed out his cigarette with quick, short jabs. "Some time ago, I think. Yes. Some time ago."

"How long?"

"In the boardroom. It was a meeting to discuss marketing a new product. It's a good product for treating ..."

"Never mind the details. What was the meeting about?"

"The meeting? To decide whether we should try to educate doctors in the seriousness of the disease our drug would treat, or whether we should concentrate on emphasizing the uses of the drug itself."

"What's the difference?"

"If we stressed the seriousness of the disease, we should create a market for the drug. The other view was that doctors already felt the need for the drug and so we should concentrate on showing what it would do and let the market grow gradually."

"When was this?"

"Four or five weeks ago." Dieppe smoothed his hair with his right hand, preening himself. "I was called in to give my expert opinion as to the likely attitude of doctors to the two different approaches."

Masters asked, "Have you seen Mr Huth since then?"

"Oh, yes. I've *seen* him."

"Have you spoken to him?"

Dieppe almost shouted. "No!"

Masters got to his feet. He thought that if he were to press on with more questions Dieppe would either collapse or go berserk. "Thank you, Mr Dieppe. I won't keep you from your work any longer."

Dieppe stared in surprise. When he realized the interview was over he helped himself to another cigarette. He was lighting it when Masters turned at the door and said: "Do you ever take sedatives?"

Dieppe said, "No, never."

"Not even when you have migraine?"

He waved the cigarette airily. "Oh, I do then, of course. That's medicine."

Masters walked away wondering just how much faith he could put in Dieppe's word. A man in so nervous a state was liable to say anything that came into his head, particularly if he thought it would benefit him in some way. Would a truthful man have said he never used sedatives if he had recourse to them as often as Dieppe suffered migraine attacks?

* * *

111

Masters joined Hill in Huth's office. "I'm not sure whether I got the truth out of Dieppe, but I had no proof of lies to confront him with, and I daren't try to break him down. He'd have caved in completely. Any joy from the tapes?"

"Nothing on Torr and Hunt, but Dieppe's definitely been sacked."

"What?"

"It's all there. A memo telling Torr to give Dieppe a month's notice." Hill handed Masters a sheet of flimsy. "I got the Krick to type you a copy."

Masters read: "As a result of your report to me and subsequent conversations with those most closely concerned, I have decided that we no longer require the services of Mr E. W. Dieppe. Please inform Mr Dieppe of this decision formally in writing, and personally ensure that he receives not only the usual month's salary and all superannuation benefits, but also a redundancy payment of one week's salary for every year of service with the Company.

"The post of Company Pharmacist will be filled from within the Company. You may, however, find it necessary to recruit a younger pharmacist to fill the gap. Please consult Dr Mouncer before taking action on this point."

Masters considered the memo for several seconds. Hill said, "He made it clear enough, didn't he?"

"Clear enough as a declaration of his intentions. But it's a paradox, all the same."

"How?"

"Sacking an old servant is a dirty trick, even in business. Sending him off with all that extra pay is generous. Dieppe's been here donkey's years, so it'll be a tidy sum."

"These bosses get like that sometimes. A rush of remorse as they're knotting the rope on the neck. But they go on tying, and the bloke's left inside, just the same."

Masters sat in one of the easy chairs and put the memo on the coffee table. He said: "That may be one explanation, but all our investigations so far show that Huth never bothered himself with hiring and firing people as lowly as Dieppe."

"He did this time, all right."

"Because of an adverse report from Torr. Have you found it?"

"I've looked, but it's not here."

"Has Miss Krick ever seen one?"

"I've asked her. She says she hasn't. But if it was marked private and confidential she says Huth would have opened it himself."

"I want it found."

"If it exists. Couldn't it have been a verbal report?"

"I don't think so. Torr hadn't spoken to Huth for some time, or so he said."

"If we can believe him."

"I'm inclined not to. But why should he lie about that?"

Hill said, "He had to. If he wanted you to believe he hadn't been given a rocket by Huth about that Metathiazanone, he had to say they hadn't spoken to each other for ages."

"Probably. But if that report was in writing and it can't be found, it looks bad for Dieppe."

"Meaning he pinched it to destroy all evidence of his motive, when he came in to plant the poison? And he didn't know about the tape?"

Masters said, "That's not the only solution. Huth said he had conversations with those most closely concerned. I can't see that anybody was more closely concerned than Dieppe himself. And yet he says Huth didn't speak to him."

Hill said, "If Huth told Dieppe he was going to give him the boot..."

Masters interrupted: "We'll ask Miss Krick if she can remember Dieppe coming to see Huth at any time during the past week."

As he passed through the P.A.'s office, Green and Brant walked in. Masters said, "Wait for me. I shan't be long, then we'll go for lunch."

Miss Krick couldn't remember a visit by Dieppe. She said, "But that doesn't mean he didn't come. I'm in and out of the office quite a lot sometimes. Mr Huth could send for anybody and speak to them while I was away."

Masters and Hill left her. Hill said, "Do you think Huth might have sent her off on some job to give him the chance of sending for Dieppe secretly? It wouldn't take long to fire him."

After lunch, when they had returned to Huth's office, Green reported on his interviews with Reculver and Pitt, and then he and Brant were shown the memo.

Green said, "I reckon we've got four suspects."

"Four?" Masters asked. "Who've you added? It was three this morning."

"I've added Dr Mouncer."

"I wondered when you'd get round to him."

Green said, "So let's see where we stand."

"Go ahead."

"Mrs Huth first. She knew her husband was running after another woman. He sometimes stayed out at nights without telling her first. With him out of the way she'll get at least fifty thousand quid. Quite a motive for a woman who's being ignored."

Masters said, "I must ask Miss Krick if *she* ever kept

114

Huth out all night. She does her own shopping and laundry so she probably lives alone."

"Torr second," said Green. "Huth had got to know where the missing Metathiazanone had gone. He called Torr a con man. Torr knew he would get the push. Cushy job and profitable sideline all gone. So he killed Huth to prevent it."

Masters said, "We'll have to have a word with Torr about the Metathiazanone. And I want to know what his report on Dieppe was all about."

Green went on, "Dieppe third. He's just the sort of nervous crank to do in somebody who's done him dirt. Huth gave him the push, so Dieppe uses the weapon he knows most about and poisons Huth before the news of the sacking becomes known."

Masters said, "Men are sacked daily, but the bosses aren't murdered."

"Dieppe had good reason. He knew he'd never get another Company Pharmacist's job. He'd have to go into a retail shop, which we know he hates; and he wouldn't get as much money there, either. So he panicked and used drugs to poison Huth."

Masters filled and lit his pipe.

Green said, "Dr Mouncer fourth. With Huth out of the way he becomes boss. I'll bet there's a difference of thousands a year in the salaries. And there's the power that goes with the job. Mouncer might think that an expert doctor shouldn't have to knuckle under to a layman. And don't forget Mouncer is the only one who knew Huth was taking Nutidal. And he's in a position to get any drugs he wants at any time with no questions asked."

Green sat back and looked at Masters, challenging him to disagree. Masters didn't give him the satisfaction. Instead he said: "You've given us something to

115

think about. And something to do. Let's get on with it. Hill, ring the Yard and get the pathologist's report. Then try to find Torr's report on Dieppe. Brant, you find out who the Huths' family doctor is and ask if he ever prescribed phenobarbitone for any of them. And get to know what he's giving Mrs Huth for that bad leg of hers."

Green asked: "What d'you want me to do?"

"I thought you'd like to be with me when I tackle Torr. But I want to see Miss Krick first."

They found Miss Krick busy with the last of Huth's dictation. She was in a happier mood. Masters guessed that getting the correspondence finished was a load off her mind. She was girlish and gay, reacting against her former mood. She said, "I don't know what's going to happen to me, but I think I could really make myself quite indispensable here if I tried. There are so many little bits and pieces to sort out I could make them last for months."

Masters said: "Hasn't Dr Mouncer spoken to you about your future?"

"Nobody's said a word to me about anything. Even the girls aren't speaking to me."

Masters wasn't surprised. Joan Parker had hinted that Miss Krick had pulled her rank as Huth's P.A. and now Huth was no longer alive, Krick's standing wasn't what it had been. He thought the girls were getting a bit of their own back by ignoring her. She probably deserved it.

He said: "Don't worry. I'm sure your job will be safe."

She replied: "I could get another tomorrow, as easy as winking, but I've got a nice flat near here. I wouldn't want to leave it and move into London."

"Did Mr Huth ever spend the night at your flat?"

She flushed. Masters thought she didn't like being reminded she had been the dead man's mistress.

"Never."

"Did he ever want to?"

"I wouldn't have let him if he had. What would the neighbours have said?"

"Quite a lot, probably. But I expect they saw him when he called on you there."

"He never came to my flat. You've got it all wrong. I told you. He sometimes needed me—or said he did—to go to conferences with him to take notes. That's all. I told you it didn't happen often."

"That makes some things a bit clearer."

"How?"

"It explains why you were not here to ring up Mrs Huth to say her husband would be away unexpectedly, if he hadn't managed to tell her himself before he went."

She looked bewildered. "I was always told well in advance that we were going. Several days, usually."

Masters sensed she was telling the truth. He was thinking hard as he and Green went to the lifts.

"Torr?" Green asked.

"Yes. Let's see how *his* pulse beats this afternoon."

Torr was in a mid-grey, smooth flannel, with covered buttons. A piece of red silk, which Masters guessed was glued to a card to fit the breast pocket, gave a splash of colour. He was writing when they entered his office. He pointedly hid the paper beneath the blotter when he saw who his callers were. He appeared, however, to be more in control of himself than Masters had expected. Masters wondered why, and came to the conclusion that Torr had probably expected to be questioned about the Metathiazanone the previous afternoon. As this had not happened, Torr had probably jumped to one or other of two erroneous conclusions. That the police had been fooled by the keys and had not found the drug, or if they had found it, they had not realized

117

its significance. Such optimism, Masters decided, deserved to blossom a little longer. Torr's fall, when it came, would be the harder. So before he began to speak, Masters sat and filled his pipe. When it was drawing satisfactorily he said: "I've just heard a taped memo from Mr Huth to you. He said you'd made an adverse report to him about Mr Dieppe. What did you say in it?"

Torr leaned back—the perfect personnel manager now. "It was a written complaint, based on Dieppe's poor attendance record and my assessment of his management potential."

"Which you believed to be poor?"

"Abysmal. How he got there is beyond me. His promotion was before my time, of course."

"I'd like to see the copy of the report."

"I'm afraid there is no copy. Confidential reports of this sort are handwritten by the people initiating them. A.A. would not allow duplicates to be made. He said it was unwise to allow typists of any grade to be privy to such things concerning their superiors; and he also wouldn't allow anything damaging to an employee's career to go on permanent record until the matter had been fully investigated and confirmed."

"And if it was confirmed?" asked Masters.

Torr corrected him: "If it *were* confirmed, the most likely result would be that the employee would be dismissed and the complaint destroyed. If investigation proved the complaint to be groundless, the paper was to be destroyed for the sake of the person who had written it as much as for the good of the employee reported on."

Green growled, "So that no chap you'd reported on could find out you'd tried to put the skids under him. Isn't that what you really mean?"

Torr ignored Green. He said to Masters: "You must see it was a very wise policy."

Masters said, "It shows *Mr Huth* was a very humane man. Now, I'd still like to know what was in your report on Dieppe."

As though he were about to open negotiations on some big deal, Torr became confidential. He said: "Part of my job is to ensure good time-keeping and attendance."

Masters remained silent. Green glowered. The hostility communicated itself to Torr, who immediately went on the defensive. "It's no use disguising the fact we're soft-hearted in the way we treat our staff. Nobody has to punch a clock."

Masters asked, "How do you keep check?"

"We use quite a simple method. In each department is a signing-in book for junior staff. The managers are supposed to rule off and sign at nine o'clock each day. They never do."

"Why not?"

"Because the senior staff is slack. We impose no check on them, and so they are not fully aware of the need to do a full day's work for a full day's pay. Most of them incline to the view that if we trust the junior staff they will repay the trust by getting to work on time. That is a myth. Ninety per cent of all our employees are up to ten minutes late each day, and the only time they are ahead of the clock is at five fifteen in the afternoons."

Masters asked: "Was Dieppe consistently late?"

"Let us say patchy. He's an unpredictable driver and his performance in traffic varies with his moods. So though he may set off from his house in good time, he's not always here on the dot."

"How do you know, if you don't keep check?" asked

119

Green. "Do you keep a special lookout for anybody you want to shop?"

Torr looked at Masters. "As you see, my office window overlooks the main entrance."

"You stand there at nine o'clock?" asked Masters.

"If he's here himself by then," said Green.

Torr snapped: "It was not Dieppe's time-keeping I complained about mostly. It was his attendance record."

Green asked: "If you don't check time-keeping how can you check on attendance?"

Torr continued to address Masters. "Every Friday afternoon the senior secretary in each department fills in an absentee report for the week."

Masters said: "Dieppe's name appeared fairly often?"

"That's the point. It never did. He took care to see that his migraine absences, which lasted anything from half a day to two days, were never included. He gave his secretary orders not to mention them."

"On what excuse?"

"Either that recurrent illness for migraine is not absence, or that the form was meant for absences other than illness. Whichever it was he was wrong."

"So you had no proper record of Dieppe's absences to show to Mr Huth?"

Torr preened himself. "Ah!" he said, "There's very little goes on in Barugt House that I don't get to hear about."

"I'll bet," said Green. "A grass on every floor. Women narks who ferret out little bits and pieces and then come gossiping to you. Some poor devil ten floors up says something about his boss and you hear about it inside five minutes. That's how it works, isn't it?"

Torr answered: "My department has to rely for much of its information on what it hears. It's common sense to keep one's ear to the ground."

"Just you tell me," growled Green, "how you could possibly keep an exact tally of Dieppe's days off unless you were told directly by another employee, close enough to him to know all his comings and goings."

Torr appealed to Masters. "This is victimization. Every word I say is wilfully misinterpreted."

Masters said, "I shouldn't worry. But don't try to hoodwink us about sources of information. We've lived with them for years. And Inspector Green's right. We usually get our information from unsavoury characters who give it in return for some favour. I've no doubt you repay your informants in some way. Now get on and tell me about your memo to Mr Huth."

Torr looked sulky. Masters thought he wasn't used to being thwarted. It showed he reigned supreme, dictating to his own department and probably the whole Company. And, presumably, as long as he did what he did in Huth's name, whether he was exceeding Huth's instructions or not, he would rarely be bothered by senior management. His guess was that Torr had a veneer of charm when all was going his way. He could probably slap a fellow employee on the back while opposing a pay increase for him. At the moment, however, Masters thought Torr was giving them a glimpse of himself in the part of management's bully. Masters didn't like what he saw. For once he found himself on Green's side.

Torr said: "I simply listed Dieppe's absences..."

"You're sure you didn't make capital out of the fact that they had not appeared on the weekly absentee lists?"

Torr reddened. "I mentioned it."

"But you never thought to warn Dieppe months ago that he was interpreting Company policy wrongly and that he should include his days off?"

"I'm not here to tutor senior staff."

"I should have thought it would have come within your welfare duties. Keeping people happy. However, what else was there in the report?"

"I gave a few instances when, in my opinion, Dieppe had not shown the initiative and grasp we in Barugt expect of executives. I suggested we had been mistaken in promoting him to his present position, and that we should be even more mistaken to keep him on."

Green said, "That's rich, that is, coming from a man who's been with the firm about a quarter as long as Dieppe, and holding only the same management rating. What bloody right had you to send in a report like that?"

"Cut it out," Masters said to Green. And then to Torr: "Did Mr Huth discuss the report with you?"

"I heard no more about it after I'd sent it to A.A."

"Not at all? What about when Mr Huth sent for Dieppe's file?"

"Nothing about the report was mentioned."

"But you guessed the two were connected."

"Perhaps."

Green said: "Yesterday you denied having any knowledge of why Mr Huth sent for those three files."

"I had no definite knowledge. My suspicions and opinions don't count."

"They don't," said Masters. "Unless you really did know why Mr Huth wanted Dieppe's file, and you wanted to avoid the suggestion that he had called for your file to mete out the same treatment to you."

"Why should he?"

"It was unusual for Mr Huth to interest himself in the staff. Yet one day recently he called for three files. Dieppe's to sack him for reasons provided by you. Hunt's because he had written a memo which as good as said the Company's publicity policy was no good. Two of the three for the high jump! Why not the third?"

"I still say he had no reason to think of dismissing *me*."

Green said: "Oh no?"

Torr flushed angrily. Masters said: "There's a little matter of a thousand Metathiazanone tablets which went missing, and have since been found in your private cage."

"And don't let's pretend you took them for a joke or to teach Mr Pitt a lesson," said Green savagely, "because it won't wash."

There was no time for Torr to think of an excuse. He had been led straight to the water. "A.A. couldn't have known anything about that," he said wildly.

Masters said: "He knew all about it. A copy of the memo from the factory saying it was missing was sent to him. On the day that memo reached him he made a note on his desk diary to ask *you* about he drug's disappearance. He linked your name with it immediately. And even more significant, the note is there with similar notes about Dieppe's shortcomings and Hunt's outspoken and unasked for memo on publicity. You were all three in his mind together, and he sent for all your files."

Torr sneered. "If that's your case, it's pretty thin. A.A. wouldn't have done anything but give me a mild rocket for lax security at the loading bay. He wouldn't have sacked me because he couldn't have known where the tin of pills had gone; and in any case he wouldn't have begrudged me a few tranquillizers for my own use, even if he had known I'd got them."

Masters said quietly, "And I don't suppose he would have minded you sending some to your friends like Dopey Cordner for stopping dogs with."

There was no fight in Torr. The remark had felled him. Masters had expected denials and lies. There was nothing. It seemed as if Masters had been right and Torr had deluded himself he was safe because no move had been made against him for twenty-four hours. Or perhaps, Masters thought, Torr must have known, subconsciously, that all was lost, and for the past twenty-four hours had been conditioning himself to accept the inevitable when it came. Masters couldn't make up his mind which had occurred; but he was pleased Torr had caved in so meekly.

"Because I've helped to dope a few dogs doesn't mean I murdered Huth," said Torr.

"Maybe not. But I've got evidence that Mr Huth was intending to discuss the missing drug with you. I've only got to show that he knew you'd stolen it and the case against you could be made to look as black as the hobs of hell. You see, Mr Torr, motive counts for a lot with a jury, and when they heard of why you wanted the Metathiazanone..."

"I tell you I haven't seen A.A. for weeks."

"That appears to be a common complaint in Barugt, so I'll accept it for the moment. But I warn you, I shall try to prove you wrong, and if I can manage it, I shall have good grounds for thinking you took another, more lethal drug from the loading bay and used it for killing Mr Huth. Is that clear?"

"Yes."

"Then my advice to you is to make a full and truthful statement to Inspector Green."

"Is he going to arrest me?"

"You'll be arrested by somebody from the local police who'll be here before you've finished the statement." Masters turned to Green. "I'll send Brant down to help and ring Superintendent Bale. He'll send somebody along."

Brant stayed long enough to make a brief report before he went to join Green. The Huth family doctor had never prescribed phenobarbitone or any other barbiturate for any member of the family. Mrs Huth had a simple vasospastic condition of the leg with slight ulceration. For this the doctor had prescribed a well-known vasodilator, not made by Barugt, which had no known side effects and the toxicity of which was so low that doses of up to twenty times the normal therapeutic level had resulted in no ill effects.

The pathologist's report confirmed that Huth had been suffering from nephritis recently. He had taken large amounts of alcohol and phenobarbitone. Both were inadvisable in his condition, and though the phenobarbitone had caused death, it had been potentiated by the alcohol. Without the alcohol he might have lived. He had died in the early hours of the morning.

With no fresh news from either of these reports, Masters was for the moment undecided what to do. But not for long. He told Hill he was going down to the main entrance to speak to Mablethorpe.

He said to the commissionaire: "Can you leave your post for a few minutes?"

"I'll get a relief. Bert, one of the internal postmen, usually stands in. I'll just see if he's free."

Masters strolled out through the double doors and waited in the open air. When Mablethorpe joined him he asked: "Army?"

"W.O. two in the Gunners. Field Artillery. Never with anybody else—Ack Ack, Anti Tank and the like."

"Yesterday morning I thought you seemed upset at Mr Huth's death. Did you like him that much?"

"I thought a hell of a lot of him. When old soldiers came into civilian life there's some who won't take them on their merits. Think because a man's been a sar' major he'll want to turn the place into a training depot overnight, or that he must be a nut case for having joined up at all. Mr Huth wasn't like them. When I applied to come here, Torr was not for having me. Thank God Mr Huth was about at the time."

"What happened?"

"The Company was just moving in here from some old premises in London, and the directors and some of the managers were down here for the day making plans. Torr came and gave me my interview here and I could tell he'd turned me down. Him and me didn't see eye to eye, but he said he'd let me know, which meant napoo in my book. Anyhow, there wasn't anybody here to make themselves useful, so I buckled to and lent a hand. I'd nothing else to do. Not that I really did as much as a Wrac on jankers, but it appears I helped Mr Huth. I didn't know who he was, but I saw him wandering about wanting this and wanting that and nobody to get it for him. Anyhow, I must have done what he wanted, because when we'd finished he asked who I was. I thought to myself 'now's my chance.' So I told him."

"And got yourself the job? Well done."

"And fifty bob for my trouble. Not that Mr Huth was free with his money. I'd say he was a bit tight-fisted, but he was like a good C.O. in the army. Never interfered, but knew what was going on by instinct. He spoke to me every time he passed me, and he called me Mister Mablethorpe. Some of 'em here don't seem to think either's necessary."

"Did you ever meet Mrs Huth?"

"I did, sir. A fine lady. Not what you'd call a pin-up girl in one sense, but a pleasure to meet at any time. She always remembered me at Christmas, and always the same message: 'For helping Adam.'"

"Has she been to Barugt House recently?"

"She only ever came about twice a year, and one of

those was always to present the prizes at the kiddies' party. She didn't fuss around like some of the other wives. I sometimes have a foyer full of them on Friday afternoons. A firm's just like a regiment, sir. If you let them, some of the wives would take over."

Masters stood in silence for a moment and then asked: "Did any strangers call at Barugt House on Monday?"

"Several. They do every day. But not one gets past me or Bert. We hold them in reception, phone up the one they want to see, and make them wait till they're fetched."

"That's at the main door. What about the other entrances?"

"We see to that, too. The back door comes in at first floor level and leads straight into the post room, and Bert or one of his mates is always there to ask questions. Nobody's supposed to use it who isn't authorized, so they know who to let through and who not. And then there's the lower door, which goes straight down a ramp into the stock room, and that's always manned. We never leave it open and empty, no matter what happens."

"Isn't there a loading bay?"

"Ah, you can get into the bay itself easy enough from outside, but it's only open for an hour or so a day. Just long enough to unload and load up again. And to get out of it on the inside's a different matter. You have to pass through a glass-walled office that always has somebody in it when the doors are open. No, I don't think unauthorized people would get very far without being seen. They might, if they were trained at getting in, but I don't think they'd be able to choose their time to suit themselves. They'd have to do it when somebody's back was really turned."

Masters said: "One of my sergeants made a remark about how difficult he thought it'd be for a stranger to get very far in Barugt House. He had to take a sheet from the women's rest room and he came back feeling like a thief because so many people had eyed him with suspicion."

"There you are then," said Mablethorpe. "If you're thinking somebody from outside killed Mr Huth, you're wrong. It was an inside job, definitely, and if I knew who'd done it, his feet wouldn't touch the ground. What beats me, though, is the reason for it. Still, you never know. These days there's plenty who'll excuse murder, rape or anything else. And the youngsters do just what they fancy."

"You don't approve of modern youth?"

"Of course I do. Most of them. I've got kids of my own nearly grown up. No, it's only the odd one that gets on my tits. They're like a gun that's firing short in a barrage. They need to be sorted out and relaid good and proper. That's what we should do with what they call social misfits. Only I don't call them that."

"Would you put them in the army, Mr Mablethorpe?"

"Not likely. That's always the cry. Put them in the army! The army can't afford them any more than the rest of the community. Good homes, hard work and short haircuts are what most of them need."

They walked towards the main doors. "Can I ask how you're getting on?" said Mablethorpe.

"Quite well, I suppose," said Masters. "But we don't know who the murderer is yet." They went inside and, for the record, Masters asked Bert if he'd noticed any strangers on Monday. The answer was no.

Bert went off to finish sorting the post. Mablethorpe said, "I've been glad of the chat, and I'd like to say sorry for yesterday morning. I was feeling a bit bloody-minded at the time."

"I could tell."

"I knew you could, else I wouldn't have said sorry now. I hate violence, you know. Of any sort."

Masters laughed. "That's the hallmark of the true soldier," he said, and pressed the lift button.

Masters and Hill waited for Green and Brant. They came to Huth's office at half past five.

Green said: "We kept him till everybody had gone and the coast was clear. But that chap Mablethorpe was still in the foyer and I didn't like the look he gave Torr. When he saw we were escorting him out, the old boy looked as though he'd have liked to have had a bash at him."

"What did you do?"

"I just shook my head, hoping the old boy would cotton on that we hadn't got him for murder yet. He understood."

Masters said: "Mr Mablethorpe is a very understanding man."

4

After the fine, bright weather of the preceding two days, with no sign of a cloud blanket to keep the ground warm at night, there was a crisp frost—the first of the autumn—on the Thursday morning. Motoring in traffic was difficult. Drivers who hadn't encountered similar conditions for at least half a year seemed taken by surprise, and out of practice at holding the road. Masters, anchored by his bulk, sat unmoving in the car. Green hung on to the back of Brant's seat till his knuckles showed white with the strain. There was little conversation except for appreciative remarks from Masters about the trees which, almost leafless, sparkled prettily in the misty but powerless sunlight. Green didn't reply. He concentrated on weaving his body with the movement of the car. He found no beauty in the midst of danger. He began to look happier only when they reached Huth's office and he could relax his tensed muscles.

"What about Torr?" he said. "Are we going to concentrate on him?"

"Forget him," Masters answered. "Cross him off your
list of suspects."

"What? How can you be sure?"

"I can't, absolutely. But I'm satisfied Huth didn't know
about Torr's dog track capers. If he *had* known, Torr
would have been out on his neck last week, not sitting
in his office this Monday plotting murder. And if Huth
didn't know, Torr had no reason to murder him."

"Hell," said Green. "You're easily satisfied. Remember Huth called for Torr's file. How do you explain that?"

"He called for Hunt's file, too. To promote him. He
might have wanted to promote Torr."

"That slob? I thought Huth was a good businessman!"

"So he was. It doesn't mean he had a perfect team.
Besides, we're all blind to other people's faults at times."
He spoke with feeling. He'd had Green round his neck
for long enough. He added: "Or learn to live with them
even if we don't accept them."

"Huth called Torr a con man."

Masters sat back and lit his pipe. Then he said, "It
seems strange to me that an important firm like this
had only a lowly departmental manager in charge of
the Personnel activity, when it includes recruiting top-
grade technical staff. Departmental manager isn't as
high as Area manager. You remember what Miss Krick
told me when I got her to talk about status in Barugt?
She mentioned one appointment at the top of the tree
among managers—just below director level. She called
him a Controller. The proper title is Control Manager.
That's what I think Huth's note was referring to. His
"Con Man" was a shorthand form of Control Manager,
and I think he intended to promote Torr. It seems a
more likely interpretation than a written reference to
Torr as a con man. Don't you think so? Bearing in mind

131

that Huth had a reputation for getting rid of people within the hour if they crossed him."

Green said: "I suppose you're right."

"One gone, two to go," said Hill.

"You mean," said Green, "that Torr was telling the truth when he said that Huth's note about the missing drug only meant that he wanted security in the loading bay tightened up?"

Masters said: "That's my opinion. Huth couldn't have cared less about thirteen pounds' worth of harmless drugs. It would have been a different matter if Meta-thiazanone had been a dangerous product."

"You're the boss," said Green. "At least Torr's inside with enough evidence against him to keep him there for a bit. Who do we look at now? Dieppe?"

"We'll go and see him before he starts dashing about the place."

Green said: "If he's in yet."

Masters and Green went to Pharmacy. The girls of the department were gathered in a group at one of the windows. They were excited, chattering and peering out onto the employees' car park far below. Catherine Blake was the first to notice them. She said sombrely: "We've got our little something to talk about."

Masters was worried by her tone. "What's happened?"

"Teddy crashed his car just outside the main gate. Look! They're pushing it into the car park now."

They peered through the gap at the bottom of the swing window. The mist was not strong enough to hide the four men manhandling a grey Morris 1000 into a corner space. The car was still a mover although the front was badly battered and, to judge by the antics of the pushers, the steering linkage damaged.

"That's just the car I'd have said he'd have had," Green said quietly. "Same type, same colour. Is he badly hurt, does anybody know?"

132

"Not really," said Vera. "Vi heard he'd got a broken arm and some cuts on his face. Somebody else heard he was unconscious."

Christine Blake said: "He had a seat belt, but he was the world's worst driver."

"And the frost caught him napping?" asked Masters.

"Fast asleep, more likely. We all knew he'd hit something one day. We've been expecting it. How he's survived as long as he has is a mystery to us."

"Where is he now?"

"I heard an ambulance, so I expect he's gone to the local hospital."

Masters and Green left. Green said: "That's the second suspect off our hands. Are you going to the hospital?"

"Not yet. We'll leave the poor devil alone for a bit. I don't want to hound him if he's ill. Brant can find out where he is and make regular enquiries. I feel I must have contributed to his crash. He was in such a nervous condition after I'd spoken to him."

Surprisingly, Green said: *"Before* you spoke to him."

"Thanks. Before I spoke to him, perhaps, but my questions can't have helped a man like that."

"Be your age," said Green, as if ashamed of his support for Masters. "He was agitated before we ever came. That means he'd already had some sort of shock."

"Like unexpectedly getting the sack?"

"And murdering his boss. That type lose their heads and do something daft that they're sorry about later. Then they can't cope mentally and so they crack up. It's as good a sign of guilt as if they'd tried to run away."

"Which is what they actually do. I know they don't take off physically, but they do mentally. I see your point. But we can't act on it. We'd better see if Mouncer can tell us anything."

Dr Mouncer's office was as big as Huth's. Instead of

a traditional desk he had three curved pieces which fitted together and enclosed him in a horseshoe. His phones were to the left, his Grundig to the right. The "in" and "out" trays were sunk below the level of the top so that slides could be drawn over them and locked for security. On the walls were framed French market scenes with the red and yellow awnings of stalls predominant. The coffee table, surrounded by club chairs, held a pale green carboy containing a miniature rock-garden. There was also a four-foot safe and above it an old-fashioned fiddle barometer and thermometer combined. Mouncer sat like a well-groomed spider at the centre of his web. He didn't rise as they went in. He said, rather ungraciously: "Good morning. Didn't my P.A. tell you I was busy?"

Masters said: "So am I."

"Obviously. You're up before your clothes are on this morning. Going the rounds before a quarter past nine! You must understand that a Company of this size has to be kept working even though your investigation is important. I came in especially early to deal with my correspondence. I should prefer to finish it without interruption."

"Investigations of this sort take precedence. Too many people are involved to risk any delays. I'd be obliged if you'd put your work on one side for ten minutes or so."

"If you insist. How can I help you this time?"

Mouncer lit a cigar and leaned back. Masters felt a surge of mistrust and dislike. Again he wondered whether Mouncer was naturally supercilious or whether he assumed the pose because he was unsure of himself. If so, why? He knew Green would be taking the worst possible view, seeing Mouncer's half-lidded eyes and thinking this man considered himself one hell of a tit. Green always jumped to superficial conclusions. That was Green's main fault as a copper. That and his everlasting sense of grievance with everything and every-body.

Masters said: "I wanted to speak to Mr Dieppe this morning."

"And now you can't unless you visit him in hospital."

"You've obviously heard."

"A minute ago. He crashed on his way through the gate, which meant, fortunately, that he wasn't going so very fast. I shall know a little later whether or not his doctors will allow you to question him today."

"It may not be necessary." Masters swung round one of the club chairs and signalled to Green to do the same. Mouncer took this pointed reference to his lack of good manners without remark. When he was comfortably seated, Masters said: "You'll probably do instead."

"Do?"

"As a substitute for Dieppe. As Medical Director you're responsible for Pharmacy, aren't you?"

"Among other things, yes."

"Which makes you Dieppe's immediate superior."

"Yes."

"Mr Huth would, therefore, have consulted you about Dieppe's performance as a manager. Sometime in the last week."

"How the devil do you know that? And what's it got to do with your investigation anyway?"

"Please answer. Did Mr Huth speak to you about Dieppe?"

"He did. And I was very cross about it."

"Why?"

"Because Torr had initiated an adverse report about Dieppe. Torr may be Personnel Manager, but that doesn't give him *carte blanche* to interfere in the internal work-ings of departments. If a complaint about the Company Pharmacist had to be made to the chairman, I was the one to make it."

135

Masters sympathized with Mouncer's anger. The doctor was not one to suffer interference from one of Torr's calibre lightly.

Mouncer went on, getting more angry at the memory: "For several years now, when the annual reviews of personnel have taken place, I've resisted attempts by the board to promote Dieppe to Control Manager. I've always agreed that a post as important as that of Company Pharmacist should carry very senior rank, but I knew that Dieppe was not fitted for promotion."

"But you kept him on, doing the job."

"Of course I did. We can't all be captains of industry or administrative wizards, and be dismissed if we're not. It would be a poor lookout for a great many people if that ever became the national policy, no matter what slurs are cast against management. The just adequate person is here with us, now. And always will be. We can't discard him. Dieppe is an adequate pharmacist, completely steeped in our methods of work here—successful methods, I assure you. If I were to get rid of him, what do you think I should get in his place?"

"Just another adequate pharmacist?"

"Right. One who would take years to become as familiar with our ways and policies as Dieppe is now. I know, because I've been trying for heaven knows how long to get a really good male pharmacist to understudy Dieppe. But I haven't succeeded. The young ones who are good enough want to move on after a year or two. The older ones who would be suitable are already settled. I've recognized ever since I've been here that Dieppe is not ideal, and I've shown it by not allowing him to be promoted above his ceiling; but I've also recognized that he's not so useless as to merit dismissal."

"Didn't you explain your views to Mr Huth?"

"At length, and in detail, on more than one occasion."

"But he ignored your advice and last week decided to sack Dieppe?"

"After lunch with a doctor who's a consultant on migraine." Mouncer frowned slightly. "I don't want you to misinterpret A.A.'s action. He went to the trouble to ask the views of a great authority. An expert. A.A. did what he did from the best and kindest of motives."

Green said: "Giving a chap the boot hardly seems kind."

"Perhaps not, superficially. A.A. pointed out that my arguments in favour of keeping Dieppe were just as damaging against him. If Dieppe, after all his years with the Company, wasn't fit for promotion, he should make way for somebody who was. That's by the way. What really sealed the issue was the idea implanted in A.A.'s mind by this consultant that a chronic migraine sufferer often benefits from taking a less exacting job. A.A. felt we were probably putting too great a strain on Dieppe, and that if he were to be dismissed he could take a less responsible job. His migraine would get a chance to disappear, and he'd be a much happier man. That's where the kindness on A.A.'s part came in. Misplaced kindness, perhaps. But there you are."

Green said: "Why give him the sack? Wouldn't it have been even kinder to keep him on and give him an easier job?"

"What as? No, Inspector. Demotion to a man like Dieppe would be such a blow to his pride that it might produce all manner of unpleasant mental reactions. Think how you'd feel if somebody junior was promoted above you."

Green scowled. Masters looked away. There was a moment of awkward silence. Mouncer had really touched a sore spot.

At last Masters said: "In your opinion, Mr Huth took

137

this action in the best interests of the man, and not those of the Company?"

"That's how I interpreted it. And knowing A.A., I'm sure I was right."

"His generosity to Dieppe substantiates that."

"Generosity?"

"We've found his memo confirming Dieppe's dismissal."

"That's how you knew? Nobody told you?"

"Nobody. You can rest assured that nobody knows, with the exception of Miss Krick. Does that make you happier?"

"Much. Because the dismissal won't stand now. But you were talking of generosity."

"It doesn't matter now."

"No. I suppose it doesn't. But if you knew Dieppe was to be dismissed, why come and waste my time in asking me?"

Masters said: "Because Dieppe says he wasn't interviewed by Mr Huth and so, as far as I know, he doesn't know he was going to get the sack. And yet he's in a very nervous state; almost one of shock."

Mouncer smiled sourly. "Shock caused by some momentous act on his part—such as murdering A.A.?"

"Maybe. I have to consider it."

"My God, you're thorough. But though Dieppe may not have seen A.A., and I don't suppose he did, he knew he was on the way out."

"You're sure of this?"

"Absolutely."

"It's important. Tell me why you're so positive."

"I told him myself. Not the terms, of course. I knew nothing of any extra payment."

"Why did you tell him?"

"Because he's one of my people." Masters was surprised. He didn't know this sort of loyalty existed in business. He suspected it was rare outside the forces. Business was a rat race. Too many people to rejoice at a dismissal, at a chance of promotion, for loyalty to flower. Mouncer rose in his estimation. Even Green showed some surprise. Mouncer went on: "A.A. wouldn't have seen him. He never saw anybody not on the board. But I view things differently. Once the decision has been taken to dispense with the services of a mature, professional man, I consider it to be unethical not to tell him so immediately, to his face, and to announce it to him by one of Torr's formal memos, which never give any reasons. A.A. was a businessman, and businessmen sometimes overlook these things. But doctors and pharmacists are ethically and professionally allied. In a place like Barugt, probably more so than outside, because we actually work together. And Dieppe was one of my managers, so I had him in here and broke the news to him. It wasn't an easy thing to do, because I knew he's emotionally unstable. But it had to be done, even though I realized I might get an unpleasant reaction."

"And did you get one?"

"Not as bad as I had feared. The poor fellow was so stunned he seemed incapable of any reaction. It was quite difficult to get him out of the office."

"When was this?"

"Last Friday afternoon."

"Was Dieppe's migraine on Tuesday the delayed reaction?"

Mouncer said rather coldly: "What you're really asking is whether his reaction to dismissal was followed by a blind hatred which caused him to kill A.A. on Monday, after which he experienced one of his normal migrainous reactions. The answer is that I can't tell you, and if I could, I wouldn't. Thank heaven I'm a

139

physician, not a psychiatrist or specialist in migraine."

Masters rose and swung his chair back into its normal position. He said: "Thank you, doctor. You've been a great help."

"You mean I've dropped Dieppe in the cart."

"That I can't honestly say."

"Can you say anything? You've arrested Torr. Not that his loss worries me, but the reason for it might. When will I be given the courtesy of an explanation?"

Masters appreciated the anger. He felt he knew Mouncer better now. He said: "An arrest is as personal a thing as a medical consultation. Torr has not been convicted. I'm not prepared to noise the matter around. However, if you can spare the time to hear him out, Inspector Green will stay and talk to you about it now."

"I'd prefer to do the talking over lunch. Will you join me in the dining-room then?"

"At what time?"

"One o'clock if that suits you. Incidentally, I told you I shall be keeping Dieppe on. This crash on top of his other troubles, or probably because of them, will just about break him. I'm going to try to see him before lunch in the hope that the good news might help his recovery. That's why I can't stay for Inspector Green now."

"You're the boss," growled Green, not quite knowing how to express his appreciation of the actions of a man who less than ten minutes before had flicked him smartly on the raw.

"For the time being," said Mouncer wryly. "The States will supersede me soon enough. And of course, you may even decide to remove Dieppe in spite of my intention of keeping him. My authority would seem to be more illusory than real."

When they were outside Green said: "He's a snooty bastard."

"You don't like him?"

"I'd say he's all right, but I really don't get it. He's what I'd call disdainful, but he's not as bad as he tries to make you think he is. He's sticking up for Dieppe at any rate, and there's not many bosses would do that. I wouldn't have minded being there when Huth and him were thumping the table at each other."

"They probably never raised their voices."

"How the hell can you fight for something without shouting?"

"You tell me. You're the left-wing pacifist. Me, I'm just an ordinary, hum-drum, take-it-as-it-comes war-monger who believes in talking quietly."

Green said: "That's all right. If you know who to talk to and when." Masters ignored this. It was a reference to his own promotion. An accusation of string-pulling.

When they reached Huth's office Hill poured them coffee from a trolley in the P.A.'s room. Green said: "Well, what about it?"

"What?"

"Dieppe getting to know last Friday he was to get the sack, and having all week-end to brood over it. He could have thought up a plan to poison Huth and then gone in to see him on Monday, pretending to beg for his job back."

Masters said: "It's a nice theory, but how did he administer the phenobarbitone?"

"In place of the Nutidal."

"How did he know Huth was taking Nutidal?"

"From Mouncer. The doc was used to discussing things with him on a professional basis."

"Perhaps." Masters picked up the internal phone. After a few seconds of conversation he put it down again. "Mouncer swears he never told anybody that Huth was taking Nutidal. I believe him. First because doctors are like that and second because Mouncer is smart enough to know that by claiming he spread the word around about Huth's Nutidal he would be diverting suspicion away from himself. And he's not doing that."

"Skip it," said Green. "Dieppe doesn't smoke cigars either, and with hands as shaky as his he wouldn't be able to do any drug juggling in that bottle without making a snarl-up, anyway."

Hill said: "We do seem to be eliminating them today. There's only Dr Mouncer and Mrs Huth left of Inspector Green's suspects."

"Elimination's useful," said Green.

"And there's nothing to stop us adding more names to the bottom of the list as we cross them off the top," said Masters.

Hill asked: "Are you changing your ideas, Chief?"

"*My* ideas? I didn't know I'd had any."

Green said: "About Mouncer..."

"Yes?" Masters held out his cup to Hill for a refill.

"He *was* in Huth's office on Monday morning; he *does* smoke cigars, and could have been carrying one of another sort same as I sometimes have a few Kensitas in one packet when I buy a packet of something else just for a change; he *did* know Huth was taking Nutidal; he *can* get any drug he wants at any time; and he's got a *motive*, as big as the Shell building—a chance of stepping into a very comfortable pair of dead man's shoes."

Masters said: "It sounds like an open-and-shut case, and I can't go as far as saying you're wrong, but it seems a little too easy to me. My opinion of this case is that it's as tough as Billy Whitlam's bulldog. You say that opportunity, motive and knowledge all point to Mouncer. Perhaps the murderer wanted it to look like the doctor's crime. If so, it's clever. But it may have happened by accident and not design. Even then it doesn't benefit us. The facts are there, but I think a clever doctor—and I'm sure Mouncer is clever, really clever—could have found a more subtle way of poisoning a victim."

Green said: "More subtle? When we haven't a clue as to how Huth was given the poison? We could get Chummy into the dock and pleading guilty, but we'd not get a verdict if we couldn't show how the phenobarbitone was administered. If that isn't subtle enough for you, what is?"

Masters agreed. "It's as odd as old Nick's hatband. But the thought had occurred to me. And lots of other little points such as where the poison came from."

Brant said: "Oh lord, in a dump like this!"

Masters turned to Green: "Take Brant and comb this bungalow from top to bottom. Discover every person who could possibly lay hands on phenobarbitone, and where they could get it. More important, find out who got some recently, and how."

"Whoever got it won't have left any leads."

"He's bound to have done. Phenobarbitone is a scheduled poison. Every grain that moves is signed for. If it isn't, there'll be a discrepancy in some accounts somewhere. Find out where."

Green and Brant left. Masters poured himself a third cup of coffee. He said to Hill: "My next port of call is to see Barraclough, the Financial Director. Hold the fort."

"You really think it's tough going?"

"You're a mind-reader! Every case reaches this stage. How long it lasts depends on luck as much as anything else. Admirable Adam! Everybody had a high opinion of him from Mablethorpe upwards." He swallowed the coffee. "Some say he was kind. Others fair-minded. As far as I can see it was true. Dieppe and Pitt haven't said Huth was kind, but he was going to give Dieppe a generous lump sum, and Pitt didn't get the rocket he should have had for losing drugs. That's generosity, too. And yet somebody hated him enough to murder him. I'd like to know why."

Masters walked from Miss Krick's door and crossed the foyer, leaving the lifts on his right. Just before he reached the swing doors he came to the single door labelled: "Mr F. Barraclough, Financial Director and Secretary Barugt Products Company." Whereas Huth in his office had always been guarded by Miss Krick, Barraclough could get into his office without entering the open-plan area and going through the financial secretariat.

Barraclough was a young, balding man, with some remnants of dark hair left, and very large brown eyes. His smile was quick and easy when he saw Masters. He jumped to his feet and came round the desk to position a chair.

"I've not really been expecting a visit, but I've been hoping to meet you." Masters immediately labelled the voice as a bit wowy, but pleasant enough. There was a slight thinness of vowel tone. "Have you resolved the problem?" Barraclough pronounced the "o" as if it were the word "owe." Masters felt it gave him an insight into Barraclough's character. What he mentally categorized as "trying to make it and damn near succeeding." He thought Barraclough's children would get it right.

Masters asked: "For any particular reason, Mr Barraclough?"

"Just curiosity." Barraclough folded the yard-long sheet of fancy ruling he was working on and leaned forward on the desk. His navy blue suit was conventional, the tie quiet enough to cause no remark. He smiled, showing a side plate in his upper teeth. "Doesn't everybody want to meet a detective from Scotland Yard?"

Masters said: "I could name a few who don't."

Barraclough laughed. "Ah, yes of course. Criminals. But what I meant was that in most people's eyes you have a very interesting job. You know, I sometimes think I'd like to be up and doing instead of just sitting here juggling with figures."

Masters said: "I find my job interesting, but then I think I have a better opinion of the force as a whole than some of the community at large seems to have."

"Most of us think the world of the police. But I agree there are too many vociferous minorities about these days. And the police make a natural target, don't they? Everything's a farce. Look at that report in the paper yesterday. The mayor of some town or other who went to jail as a conchie in the war is going to lay the wreath on the War Memorial next month. To me that's wrong. The permissives think it's all right."

Masters grimaced and lit his pipe. To his surprise Barraclough also produced a pipe. A shrinking violet of a pipe with an aluminium stem that seemed at odds with the old-fashioned tobacco jar which he took from a drawer. He said: "I have to keep it off the desk top. I use such dam' great sheets of paper in my job."

The air grew blue as they talked.

"How long have you been with the Company, Mr Barraclough?"

"Eight years. Long before A.A. took over. He made me a director six years ago, soon after he came."

"You've stayed. A lot of your colleagues have gone."

"Quite a lot."

"Why? Did they fall foul of Mr Huth? I heard that some had been edged out."

"Edged out—even nudged, but never pushed. I don't know who told you, but I'm sure nobody but me can tell you what really used to happen."

"I'd be interested to hear."

"Why? Will it help you to get inside the skin of the case?"

"Perhaps."

"As you know, we're American-owned, but, on paper at least, completely autonomous. A.A. was an excellent businessman and first-class administrator."

Masters raised his eyebrows, but didn't speak. Barraclough didn't miss it. He asked: "What's the matter? Don't you agree?"

"Shall we just say I've come across one or two things which I think might have been improved. But I'm not a businessman. I don't know about these things, so I may be mistaken."

"Of course you've found faults. A.A. knew they were there and could have put them right. Would have put them right if it would have benefited the employees, but he deliberately didn't do so for a very good reason. He believed that in the circumstances it would have been a mistake to have an absolutely perfect set-up."

"Why?"

"Because once an American-owned company in this country is as perfect and profitable as possible, the States take over direction. They know that once an operation is really established they can dispense with top management here and run the company by remote control from New York. It's happening all the time."

"You're saying that a too successful businessman can work himself out of a job?"

"Right first time. As I say, it's happened more than once. A.A. knew it, and deliberately set out to make slightly less profit each year than he could have done if he'd pulled out all the stops and decided to commit business suicide. His method of ensuring a shortfall was not to appear to be slacking, but to run a slightly imperfect machine working flat out."

Masters said: "I should have thought that would have made a nasty grating noise that could be heard all the way from here to Washington."

"A.A. knew where to put the right drops of oil to keep it quiet. This business of directors is a good example of what I mean. A.A. didn't often make mistakes in picking the right men for the board. He never had need to dismiss any of them. Quite a few have gone, however, because he used to urge them to take other openings while they were still young enough to make the change easily."

"For their own good?"

"And so that they shouldn't go down with the ship should the evil day come. He stayed himself to delay it as long as possible and because he knew he would always be able to get a decent job. With any type of firm, not just a pharmaceutical company."

"What about you?"

"Accountants are always in demand, fortunately, so A.A. never found another job for me and nudged me into it."

"He did that? Actually found jobs for people?"

"More or less. He'd got his ear to the ground. If he heard that such and such a firm wanted such and such a man, and he thought we'd got somebody who could compete, he'd suggest it and back the application to the hilt. Few people except those actually involved ever got to know. A.A. didn't want other firms to think he was using them for placing his own people. It would have looked bad."

Masters said: "Would you call him a business wizard?"

"He kept everything very close. I told you he never said a word about his deals, and he rarely saw many people here."

147

"I heard so."

"But he piloted a clever course. He managed to be so successful that the Americans had no cause to sack him. At the same time he damped down his success unobtrusively. He could do it. You know one of the American failures or weaknesses is an almost pathological faith in capital investment. If A.A. was told to achieve an increased budget, he claimed the need for more capital expenditure. That took some of the gilt off the gingerbread. At home here, if the Ministry of Health requested price cuts, he'd agree without argument if our profits looked like going too high. Otherwise he'd fight like the devil, and win. He made it appear that his hand had been forced when it suited him."

Masters was thinking that he would have preferred to meet Huth alive rather than dead. He said: "I've heard from all sides that he was a kind man."

Barraclough thought for a moment. "Don't misunderstand me. He was kind all right. But not so—what's the word? basically? intrinsically?—kind as one might have expected. His kindliness and thoughtfulness were a constituent part of his business acumen. They sprang from knowing what was the right thing to do from a business angle. They weren't part of his own, inbuilt character. He put them in. Do you follow me?"

"Quite easily," said Masters. "And I'm pleased to hear you say it. I've heard of at least one example when his action seemed out of character for a kindly man, but quite correct from the standpoint of business. Dr Mouncer hinted at what you just said."

"Did he? I'm glad of that, because as long as I knew A.A. I was convinced that if ever he were to come up against it in business, he would be as ruthless as Hitler, and his kindness would fly out of the window. In fact, I think it's true to say that he's used kindness as a weapon. He came up the hard way himself, and I suspect he used consideration just when it suited him, and not unless. But in the old days it was his own personal fight. Since he's been with Barugt it's been what you might call a corporate fight, and deep personal feelings haven't entered into it quite so much."

"A very complex character."

"In some ways. But he'll be remembered as being astute and considerate. And he was. I know he didn't do quite as much as he wanted for the staff, because to some extent his hands were tied by America. But he did his best, and that was dam' good."

They sat silent, digesting this. Masters was just about to speak again when the door from the secretariat opened. Masters could have sworn that it opened gaily. At any rate it opened wide, quickly, and then was held firmly from crashing back. Joan Parker came in. Masters didn't know whether he would have described her entry as sailing in or waltzing in. Whichever it was it was smooth and graceful, with a slight swirl of a heavily pleated skirt. Miss Parker had her lovely head set well back, which gave her an air of distinction blended with aloofness. Her breasts were high, well pronounced and firm as those of a well-carved figurehead. It was obvious she didn't see Masters there, placed as he was, and her first reaction on entering the atmosphere of Barraclough's office was to exclaim: "Phew! What a fug!" and to open a window as she said it. When she turned round and realized he was present, Masters thought she hesitated just momentarily in her progress to the desk to put down the papers she was carrying.

She said: "Really, it's too much. Two pipes going and no air in the room." As if to support her complaint the disturbed smoke, writhed into twisted clouds, began to move slowly towards the window and then gathered momentum to float out into the bright sunlight. She gave Masters the impression that she mothered Barraclough, as a top-drawer social worker might hover over a poverty-stricken family, and wasn't above ticking him off if she thought he deserved it. He almost grinned with delight when Barraclough confirmed the impression by saying: "Sorry, Joan," and laying aside his pipe.

Miss Parker said to Masters: "We meet again! How you do get about! If many detectives smoke a pipe as foul as yours there's small wonder police interviews are called 'grilling.' This office is like a kipper factory."

Masters wasn't for apologizing. He said: "Good morning, Miss Parker."

Barraclough, embarrassed, asked: "Is it urgent, Joan?" Masters felt a momentary pang of jealousy at the intimacy of Barraclough's address and his unthinking acceptance of having a girl so lovely at his beck and call.

"It can wait until later. It's the critical-path diagram for BH 3096 with the revised figures."

Masters didn't understand. He felt out of it.

Barraclough said: "Rightyho, Joan. Leave it with me and I'll have a look at it later."

Miss Parker returned to her office without another word to Masters. He had about a second in which to appreciate her lithe movement. Then she was gone. He wondered whether he had ever encountered such youthful maturity—or was it mature youthfulness? He decided she combined the charm and grace of a poised woman with the firm, physical attractiveness of a girlish Atlanta. All he knew was that Joan Parker disturbed him, and he wondered...

"She's a good P.A., too." Barraclough was laughing at him. He hoped like hell he hadn't been obvious. The thought that he might have been embarrassed him.

"I beg your pardon. I was daydreaming."

"So that's what you call it! I've been watching you. You seemed quite a long way away, though I'd put it at just the other side of the door."

Masters merely said: "Maybe."

Barraclough said: "I hope you were thinking of Joan only in connection with the case."

Masters didn't rise to this. Instead he asked: "Was Dr Mouncer aware of the way Mr Huth ran the Company?"

"He knew."

"Did he approve?"

"Unreservedly."

"Tell me how you can be so sure."

"Dick Mouncer's a clever man, but first and foremost he's a dedicated doctor."

"What's he doing in industry, then?"

"He takes the view that as a doctor here he probably has more medical influence over more people than he would have in general practice. You know, being a dedicated medical man doesn't have to mean treating measles and delivering babies."

"I should have thought a doctor needed people to doctor."

Barraclough shook his head. "Dick doesn't need people. You may have noticed he's a bit standoffish." Masters thought, and how! "Here, he rightly claims to be the medical conscience of a big and important sector of medicine. And he refuses to involve himself with anything but good medicine."

"What do you mean by that? I take it you're not suggesting some of your own products are not as good as they should be."

"Heavens, no! Dick refuses to make a claim for our products, or allow even a suggestion to be made, that has not been fully substantiated by trials investigation, controlled proof, and then endorsed in practice. He accepts *in vitro* results only as far as they point the way for *in vivo* tests.

"Even when he's got his proof he's rabidly against making our claims too specific. When we know a certain drug will be effective in certain ailments he'll never go further than saying it *may* be effective, or that it's *logical to assume* it'll be effective. His argument is that though as many as ninety per cent of patients with the same disease may be typical and will respond to the accepted drug, the other ten per cent will be atypical and will need other remedies."

Masters said: "What was Mr Huth's view of Dr Mouncer's attitude?"

"A.A. thoroughly approved. We've got a dam' fine reputation because of it, and it fitted in with A.A.'s ideas exactly. Don't you see how it worked ideally for him?"

"You tell me."

"Dick's policy of using good medicine as good promotion, instead of vice versa, meant that we avoided any dramatic short-term rises in profits, which gimmicky promotion might have got us. But it also meant we had no depressions, and so we got a smooth, regular increase. The graph rose steadily year by year. A casual glance would show you immediately that the Company was doing well. It would also show you that the end was nowhere in sight. And that's exactly the impression A.A. wanted to give."

"Was Dr Mouncer one of Mr Huth's choices?"

"One of his very best."

"Why wasn't Mouncer nudged out like the other bright boys?"

"Because doctors, like accountants, can always get another comparable job. Besides, Dick was more valuable than most for the reasons I've just given you."

"And now he's taken control."

Barraclough grimaced. "For a few days only. He won't be appointed chairman."

"Why not?"

"He doesn't want it. Even if he were asked he wouldn't accept. He's already asked the States not to consider him."

"Not even for salary reasons? And power?"

"They neither of them matter a damn to Dick. Over and above what he's got, that is."

"Which is not inconsiderable, I suppose."

"He gets five thousand a year. A.A. got fifteen. But Dick's a bachelor, with no family. No, there's nothing odd about him at all, except that more money doesn't interest him. It doesn't, you know, with some people, after a certain standard has been reached. Particularly when you're not allowed to keep much of it. Dick Mouncer isn't going about hoping for a rise of five hundred at Christmas. Annual salary reviews don't interest him. He's got everything he wants in the way of comforts. The only thing he'd go over the wall for is a useful new drug. He can never get enough of those. And as for power—well, Dick had more *real* power than A.A."

"How do you make that out?"

"A.A. laid down policy, but Dick could veto or permit the activity of practically any of the technical departments, what Publicity said, and what the reps could say to doctors. I tell you, he's interested in medicine. He's good at administrative work because he's a naturally bright boy. But he doesn't like it."

Masters said: "I want to be quite clear about the premises on which you base your opinion. Is it observation of the man over the last few years?"

"It's not just my opinion. It's fact. I've already told

you he's informed the States he doesn't wish to be considered for A.A.'s job. Some time ago he asked that the post of Medical Director should not be regarded as number two in the hierarchy."

"Whom did he ask?"

"A.A. and our President on his last visit from America. He had no luck."

"What was his reason?"

"He feels that, ethically, the business side should be divorced from the medical side. He wants to interest himself solely in the efficacy of the products and wants no hand in marketing them. His request was turned down on political grounds."

"What political grounds?"

"One of the great things in favour of the real, research-based pharmaceutical companies is that top management includes, in reality as well as on paper, experienced doctors. If this wasn't a fact, all our critics could claim we were a lot of laymen gulling doctors into using worthless drugs just for the sake of making fat profits."

"How soon will a new chairman be appointed?"

"In confidence, the man we shall get has already been earmarked by America."

"Not from within the Company?"

"We shall soon be pressing money into the palm of the managing director of one of our competitors. He may well be one of A.A.'s former lambs coming back to take over."

Masters stood up. "I'm meeting Dr Mouncer for lunch at one. Just so that I shan't be putting my foot in it, does he know everything you've told me?"

"Everything. There'll be no need to watch your tongue."

"Thanks. For the time as well as the information."

Barraclough came round from behind his desk. "I've

wanted to talk like that to somebody for a long time. Thank you for listening. I hope it helped."

"It did. Enormously. You've no idea how bewildering it can be being pitchforked into an organization like this; to take it to pieces without undoing any of the parts."

"I have. We brought in a firm of business consultants to advise us on part of our field operation. It took them three months to find *their* way round. Or, at least, that's what they charged us for."

"The fool," said Mouncer. "The blind, stupid fool. I'm not worried about Torr himself, you understand, or his racing colleagues. I'm more concerned about the greyhounds than any of them."

Masters said: "And about something else, even more important?"

"Yes. The tranquillizers. We're just beginning to find out that helpful as they are to many people, even these mild relaxants are dangerous in the wrong hands. The Dunlop Committee has just attributed over ninety deaths to them. And Torr, the thundering idiot, has been distributing them wholesale to witless thugs. You appreciate the danger, I hope?"

Masters said gravely: "You mean that because they appear to be relatively harmless—simply strong enough to sedate dogs without any ill effects—some of these people might have been eating them like Smarties."

"With the possibility of serious *sequelae*. Every little girl clerk in this organization should know better. Does know better. In fact, some of the senior typists and secretaries could give points to some doctors concerning our own products. But Torr! I'd like to flog the oaf." Mouncer's mouth set in a hard line. He picked up a spoon and attacked his chocolate mousse.

When he had finished, he dabbed at his mouth with

his napkin and went on: "There's the possibility of scandal, too. Don't smile. It's a reaction you meet every day of your life, no doubt. And it's laughable. But I want you to understand that scandal doesn't worry me for my own sake. But the reputation of this firm is above rubies. Not only for me as Medical Director and the rest who earn their bread and butter here, but for the world at large. If some physicians—and there are as many bigoted asses in their ranks as in any other walk of life—were to stop prescribing Barugt drugs because they lost faith in the Company, we should lose a few pounds in profits, but many sick people would not get the best treatment available. I say that because some of our drugs have no equals anywhere in the world."

"I'll put in a special plea for discretion to be shown," said Masters. "I'm expecting Superintendent Bale this afternoon, and I'll mention it to him. He'll do what he can."

Mouncer murmured: "Grateful. We'll get—are getting—enough notoriety over A.A.'s death. Though, to be fair, the tone of the Press is helpful and hopeful. Due, no doubt, to your being on the case."

Masters laughed. "My mother has turned herself into a press-cutting agency with only one client. We'll be moving to bigger premises any day now."

Mouncer pushed his chair back. "Don't discourage her. Her efforts must be encouraging to you, and I'm a great believer in the power of encouragement. It cures as many ills as drugs do—given the chance. And in your case I should say it serves to enhance, or at least confirm, your belief in yourself, thereby making you a better policeman."

Masters said: "You extend psychological cures into the realms of psychological success."

Mouncer said: "Don't be too cynical." He ushered

Masters to the door. "It's a proven fact that fourteen per cent of all patients involved in drug trials respond to placebos, because they're under the impression they're getting the latest—and, therefore, to them, the best—of wonder drugs. The old bromides like 'Think you can and you will' were all, to some extent, based on experiences and observations the facts of which we are only just rediscovering with the help of computers."

They went up together in the lift. Mouncer went straight to his own office. Green and the sergeants joined Masters in Huth's office.

Masters said: "I've had too good a lunch to want to move out of this chair this afternoon. What about anybody else?"

"You're all right," said Green. "You can sit here and wait for the Super. *We're* trying to find missing phenobarb. In a place like this! If we have any luck it'll be a miracle."

"You've checked the Pharmacy records?"

"Back to the year spit. All accounted for."

"And Reculver's department?"

"He's got a doctor's signature for every grain sent out since his books were last inspected. I haven't been down to see Pitt yet, but it's too much to hope that I'll be lucky with him a second time."

Masters said: "You've got to try him."

"I know."

Hill said: "I've been on to the hospital. Dieppe's comfortable, but they don't want him to be questioned just yet if we don't have to see him."

"Skip it. If the Pharmacy stock of phenobarbitone is all accounted for we'll forget Dieppe for the moment. I can't see him fiddling it from anywhere else." He turned to Green. "Can you?"

"No." It was definite. The certainty of a man whose

experience has taught him when he can be sure of things. Masters was pleased. Green was having a more co-operative phase. He thought it might even be Green's birthday and his wife had remembered to give him a present.

Masters said: "But I would like to know about the strange cigar. Have we had the report on it yet?"

"Verbal only," said Hill. "I rang last night. The full report is being typed today and you'll get it when you call in at the Yard."

"What's it going to say?"

"The cigar's a Du Plat. Pretty common these days because they're being pushed to take the place of fags. Their adverts take the line that if you're a cigarette smoker you'll find a Du Plat just as mild and satisfying as a Virginian; and they reckon that old and young of both sexes enjoy them equally. And that's about right, because I think their main sales are among the long-haired lot."

Masters sat thinking over what he'd heard before lunch from Barraclough. He'd had little time to assimilate it while listening to Mouncer's views. Bale walked in.

"Any luck?" he asked Masters.

"If you mean have we made an arrest the answer is no."

Bale peered at him and then said: "You don't look too despondent." He turned to look at the others. "But these three look pretty glum."

Hill said: "Chief Inspector Masters has spent the last two days proving that most of our suspects are innocent, sir."

Bale said: "That's what I like to hear. Rule out those who couldn't have done it and whoever's left is your man. So you see, sergeant, you're progressing."

"There's nigh on eight hundred suspects in this case," grumbled Green. "And when you've got to comb the whole lot in the hope of finding a thimbleful of phenobarb, it looks like being a long job."

Masters said: "It really is too early to tell yet. What about the inquest?"

"Person or Persons Unknown. And nothing said for you to worry about. The funeral's on Saturday."

Green and the two sergeants went off to continue their search. Masters and Bale sat down and Masters reported what had been done to date. When he had finished Bale said: "You've covered some ground. I'm surprised to hear you're not considering the Krick woman. She had the best opportunity, you know. And a motive. It's a bit difficult to believe she sat in her office all afternoon and heard no movement in here."

"From a semi-comatose man? This room is almost soundproof. We've tried it. And Krick's windows look out onto the main road. There's not a high level of noise if the windows are closed, but there's a constant background of sound from the traffic. You don't notice it unless you stop to listen, but it's loud enough to drown the noise of any weak movement in here."

Bale stood up. "I'm going before I get taught any more lessons. By the way, thanks for Torr. It was a bit of luck, Green stumbling on him like that."

Masters agreed in a dry voice. Green had lived up to his reputation for taking credit that wasn't entirely his.

Bale said: "I'm wondering if I can't get Torr for defrauding punters as well as everything else we're throwing at him. What silly idiots some men are."

Masters accompanied him to the lifts.

5

Hill had joined Green and Brant in the search for phenobarbitone. Masters was alone. For a long time he sat and thought. The smoke from his pipe turned the air a dirty grey. The pipe needed cleaning and smelt foul. After half an hour it tasted foul, too. He got up and helped himself to a glass of tonic water from Huth's stock. He was still smoking and thinking when the afternoon tea trolley arrived. In all, he sat for two hours considering the people he had met in the last three days and going over carefully in his mind what each one had said. Recalling their expressions and their attitudes, he was sweeping up facts that had fallen round him like poppy petals at a Remembrance ceremony. Now he gathered them together. Occasionally he referred to retrospective notes he had made or the copies the others had made. Finally, when he discovered he'd drunk so many cups he'd drained the pot intended for four, he took his coat from the studio couch. He put it on as he went down in the lift to look for Green. He found him talking to the woman who served in the Company shop.

"Any luck?"

"Not a skerrick," said Green. "I'm trying here, but I know they never touch dangerous stuff."

Masters said: "I'm going to see Mrs Huth. Make your way back without me when you're ready to go. Can I borrow Hill to run me to a bus stop?"

Green said: "He's about somewhere."

"Before I go, I've remembered something that might be worth looking into."

"What's that?"

"They've a display case museum outside the library on the fifth floor. Near the back stairs. It's got packets of all their drugs in it. See if the phenobarb bottle is full or empty."

Green called Brant and Hill. Brant went with him to investigate the museum.

It was nearly dark when Masters arrived at Huth's house. Mrs Huth again answered the door herself. He felt glad she hadn't gone into any form of mourning. She didn't seem surprised to see him.

This time she led him to a small breakfast room. He saw she had been using it as a general living-room. Newspapers on the chairs, correspondence and an open book on the sideboard, and a white West Highland terrier standing perkily before an open fire. "It's cosy in here," she said. "It has the only chimney in the house that isn't blocked. I insisted on having one left when the central heating was put in. I love a fire. I can only burn smokeless fuel, of course, but it glows nicely, don't you think?"

He agreed with her. The dog nosed him. It decided he could be trusted. It put its forepaws up on his knee and stretched, depressing its back in a downward curve of canine elegance.

"Down, Talcum! Silly name for a dog. He gets Tally most of the time the children are here. Sit down and have a cup of tea, Chief Inspector. It's already made. I'm indulging myself with a book and a fire."

"I don't blame you. Enjoy it while you can."

She didn't falter in pouring out the tea, but she said: "That sounds ominous."

"It wasn't meant to be. If you go back to teaching you'll be returning to discipline, with a timetable to keep to."

He thought it must be at least his sixth cup of tea that afternoon, but it was the best. He sipped it slowly, while still steaming hot. It gave her time to adjust herself to his presence, although he didn't think she really needed it. At last he said: "This is very pleasant, but I'm not here on just a social call."

"I hadn't made the mistake of thinking you were."

He said: "I called because the time has come for me to know some of the more intimate details of your life with your husband."

"Oh, dear! I'm not unusually prudish, but I do like to keep my private life to myself."

"Believe me, I understand. But I've got to ask you some more questions. I've learned a bit about Mr Huth's character. All to his credit. But I'm sure I haven't got everything I should have. I haven't had time to get round to everybody in Barugt. But it seems to me to be contrary to nature to find a man virtually without faults. And it's even more unusual to find a very successful man, who is respected by everybody, murdered in his office. I'm looking for a weakness in his character. Something that would provide somebody with a motive for murder."

"You think he must have seriously offended somebody? Enough to lead to murder?"

He said: "I can't think what fault or offence could be serious enough to warrant murder. But it seems logical to suppose that is what happened."

"Why are you so sure?"

"Because he wasn't murdered for the money he had in his pocket. As far as we can tell, no envious business competitor killed him. There are none of the usual motives like jealousy, greed and envy which spring entirely from within the brain of the murderer. So I'm assuming that the reason for the murder is to be found inside the character of the victim himself. Now it's usually fairly easy to find weak spots in the characters of people who invite murder, but with Mr Huth I can't find a weak spot. Nobody can show me a blemish worth remarking. I'm not so naive as to suppose that Mr Huth was without human weaknesses. We've all got our fair share. But none of his colleagues seems to know what they were in his case. And the only drawback *I* can pinpoint is your husband's almost pathological shyness, and I've never heard of shyness inviting murder."

"So you've discovered he was shy."

Masters said: "It shouted at me. If you go and speak to half a dozen people in Barugt House you'll learn it in as many seconds. It makes me wonder how he managed to become a successful sales manager, hating meeting people like he did."

She refilled his teacup and offered him a plate of cake. She said: "Have a piece of this. It's got nuts in. I baked it myself yesterday, just for something to do."

He took the cake and said, "Now you know why I want intimate details. Outsiders' opinions haven't got me anywhere."

She said: "I don't believe you." She said it good-humouredly.

"No?" He was neither surprised nor perturbed by her remark.

"I think you've come here—in the nicest possible way—already knowing what you want to hear."

"Perhaps. But I've still got to hear it, haven't I? And there's one other point you've missed. I've got to recognize whatever it is when I hear it."

"That's what I thought. You've gathered a lot of the pieces together, but there's one key piece missing. You know its shape and size, but not its colour."

He said, with his mouth full of cake: "More than one bit missing. That's why I've got to recognize what I want as you talk."

"All right," she said. "Where shall I start? You've learned he was shy. That's not quite right. It's a bit of a generalization, and generalizations never do hit the nail squarely on the head."

He nodded as he busied himself with the cake crumbs. Gathering them together into a little ball with the ends of his fine fingers. She watched him pop the compact wedge into his mouth and then said: "Adam was a queer mixture. I hope it doesn't sound too silly, but I'd call him a shy extrovert. He got on very well indeed with people who really liked him. And he could tell whether they did or not at a first meeting. If they did the friendship could develop very successfully. But if anybody showed dislike, or even indifference, to him, he was never able to be himself in their presence, no matter what happened later."

Masters said: "Mablethorpe."

"Who? Oh, yes, Mr Mablethorpe. He's a good example. Adam and he took to each other right from the start."

"Sorry. I interrupted you."

"That's all right. What I was about to say was that the worst of all was if somebody mistakenly looked down on Adam. Socially, I mean. Then the fat was really in the fire."

"I don't understand."

"I'll try to make it a bit clearer. Adam wasn't class conscious at all—until he was affected by it. Then he was. You know yourself how fond he and Mablethorpe were of each other, and I'm certain Adam was extremely courteous to the youngest most trollopy little girl he ever employed. He never *used* his position, and when he went to see people, other businessmen or senior civil servants, he always went unannounced, just like anybody else. But you know there's often a brash person to be got past on these occasions—somebody who is deferential to the few and tries to be superior to the many. Adam wouldn't tolerate anybody trying to be superior to him, and I'm afraid that on those occasions when it did happen, he pulled strings to take them down a peg or two. In his position he could do it."

Masters said: "I react in exactly the same way myself. And what you've said explains one point. I can see now why his workpeople who would naturally show some outward respect to their employer found him charming when they happened to meet him, even though he was often shy of them. But you haven't mentioned yourself in all this. How did you find him to live with?"

She said with a smile: "He was a good husband, but far from perfect."

He said, so that there should be no mistake: "You're not referring to untidiness about the home or other irritating habits of males who aren't too well house-trained?"

"No. About the house Adam was as good as, but no better than, the other adult males I know. I was talking about his half of our marriage partnership. Wasn't that what you wanted to hear?"

He nodded. She passed the cake plate to him again and he hesitated before taking a piece. At last he took the end slice. "I like the outside," he said. "The crispy bits."

She put the plate down and said: "We hear so much these days about how hard a couple must work to adjust themselves if their marriage is to be a success. I suppose it's right in theory, but it's not always easy to put into practice."

"It was difficult for you? Or both of you?"

"Both. Adam just couldn't adjust himself to me. I tried—I honestly did—to move towards him, and I think I managed it fairly well up to a point. But he always wanted more than I could give."

"It happens like that more often than not."

"Does it? Well, anyway, this is where I think the theory fails. Giving without spontaneity is bogus, and bogus feelings ruin a marriage as fast as, if not faster than, incompatibility. That's by the way. We were both aware of our wants and our shortcomings; but I think this is where we made our big mistake. We never discussed them."

He carefully collected a cake crumb from his knee and dropped it on his plate. He said nothing. Talcum nudged his hand and asked for the crumb.

She went on: "As I told you, Adam, for all his virility, was a bit Victorian in his attitude. He shied away when I tried to take the initiative, and he only ever mentioned the subject when goaded into it because I was feeling particularly noncooperative. Naturally, the only response he got on those occasions was far from enthusiastic."

Masters felt a bachelor's irritation for the difficulties of marriage. But he felt sympathy for Mrs Huth. Proud, wellread, and having to confess to an inadequacy she hadn't been able to overcome for all her intelligence and effort.

"We still shared the same bed," she said candidly. "These last two years I've been at the change of life, and Adam treated me with great kindness."

Masters thought that was big of him. Aloud, he said: "That was in character."

"Only partly. He really *was* a kind man, but his attitude still surprised me."

"Why?"

"It seemed contrary to nature to be able to suppress a sex drive which in him was a tremendous urge. That's why I shouldn't have been surprised if you'd found he had a mistress. Have you, incidentally?"

"Not a whisper since I spoke to you last." He stood up.

"Honestly?"

"I swear it." He picked up his hat. "Thank you for telling me all this."

"Did you recognize what you were expecting to hear?"

He looked at her for a moment. "I'll have to think it over carefully. I'd better go and do it now, before I forget what you've told me or I outstay my welcome."

"The hunt for weaknesses in Adam's character must go on." She sounded bitter. He hurried to put her right.

"I've got to keep looking. But I promise I'll not turn over more stones than I've got to. I'm not out to blacken him, you know."

"I know. Surely you see I trust you. I wouldn't have spoken to you like this if I didn't."

Masters thanked her for the tea. At the front door he stopped and said: "Do you happen to know anybody who really disliked Mr Huth?"

"At Barugt House, you mean?"

"I think it would have to be somebody there."

She thought for a moment. "No. I can't think of anybody. They would all have been weeded out long ago, knowing how Adam worked. He did so like a friendly team."

"You're sure he would dismiss anybody who didn't like him? Just for that alone? It doesn't match up with his known concern for employees' welfare."

"No, it doesn't, does it? But I think he would try to do it as gently as possible all the same ... no, wait. There is one man. Adam told me he was always being belligerent towards management. Over the question of work, of course, nothing else. Adam said he couldn't help it because he was born that way. A dour man."

"Who was he?"

"I'm trying to remember. Adam liked him in spite of everything he had said. Yes. Now I remember. Adam said that this man's suggestions were always quite logical, and any red-blooded man would get cross if for no apparent reason all his good ideas were squashed. So Adam promoted him as a sort of sop."

"No idea of his name?"

"No. But I think he must be in Research and Development. They're the people who are supposed to have ideas for products, and the impression seems to stick at the back of my mind."

"I'll find him."

"I'm sure you will. But please don't think I'm saying this man might have murdered Adam. It wasn't that sort of dislike at all. Simply business differences."

Masters said: "Please don't worry. All I want from him is a different slant on your husband's character. It's good to know both sides. Goodnight, and thank you for the cake. I enjoyed it."

He set off for the tube, trying to remember in what connection he had heard Research and Development mentioned before.

* * *

168

"No good," said Green the next morning in the car. "Half the things in that blasted museum are dummies."

Masters said: "I thought they might be, but we had to try."

"No dangerous drugs in there at all, and some of the others with what's known as a short shelf life are left out, too. All they put in the cases are the empty bottles and boxes. They're more interested in labels than contents."

"Who looks after it? The librarian?"

"Yes. She doesn't know much about the products, and the key's never been out of her possession, she says."

"We've *got* to find out where the phenobarbitone came from. And I want to trace a bottle of Nutidal as well." Green grimaced. Then he said: "You've a hope. We've tried everywhere for phenobarb without success. Now you want Nutidal. It's one of their biggest sellers, and because it's non-poisonous they don't have to get a signature for it. Yesterday we were knee deep in statistics about Nutidal samples. They plaster the countryside with the stuff. Anybody could get hold of it at any time without anybody else being the wiser."

Masters said: "We've got to have the phenobarbitone at least. The Nutidal if possible. So go to it."

"What if it didn't come from Barugt House after all?"

"You mean somebody might have got it on prescription from their own doctor."

"Why not?"

"You know the answer. If you finally fail here, you'll have to interview every employee's doctor. Take your choice."

Green didn't reply. Masters thought that would stop him grumbling for an hour or two. The sergeants kept quiet. Green brooded until they reached Huth's office. Then he said: "You didn't tell us what Mrs Huth said last night."

Masters didn't want to give them a long account. He said: "She gave me a cup of tea and some cake. Told me she thought her husband was oversexed and that somebody in Research and Development disliked him. Not enough to kill him."

Green asked: "What are you going to do now?"

"I'm going to try to help you."

"How?"

"You've exhausted every known source—or every source known to us. There's only one thing to do. Find new sources. I'll be pottering around."

Masters left them and went to Hunt's office. He pressed the handle and pushed, but the door only opened fractionally. He gave a harder push and heard a startled exclamation from inside. He recognized the voice. Vera Chambers. He peered round the door and saw her rubbing an elbow. Hunt was close to her looking embarrassed and all protective.

"Damn you," said Hunt. "Can't you knock on the outside?"

"Why? Have I knocked somebody out?"

"Only Miss Chambers. You've hurt her elbow." He gently shepherded Vera away from the door. "Oh, come in," he said in exasperation.

Masters said: "I wasn't to know you were only just inside. Sorry, Miss Chambers."

Vera laughed ruefully. "It would have been all right if you hadn't barged with all seventeen stone or whatever you weigh."

Masters said: "I always mistrust doors that won't open. You must admit it was a silly place to stand."

Hunt said: "She had no choice. I was holding her. It's all right. I was only kissing the wench."

"At this time of day?"

Vera said: "We've agreed to get engaged. Just now. Agreed, I mean."

"I see. Congratulations. But why choose this spot?"

Hunt said: "Where else? It's the most strategic point. Away from the windows so's we shouldn't be seen, and acting as a doorstop against unwanted intruders. We hadn't reckoned on a visit from you, otherwise I'd have shoved the desk across."

Masters regarded Hunt solemnly for a moment. "You're a quick worker."

"I know. I told you I was going to try my luck. Well I have, and I've been accepted."

"Well, really," said Vera, who was patting her short hair into place. "Why don't you shout it from the top floor windows?"

Masters said, smiling: "I'd want to, in his place. And take it from me he's got it badly. He couldn't even hear me mention your name without wanting to talk about you. That's a sure sign."

She blushed at his compliments and said modestly: "It's just one of those things. Now we can tell you, we might as well admit we've both had an eye on each other for ages, and we've been pretending we haven't. Last night he invited me out and had enough gumption to tell me how he felt about me. I can't think what made him take the plunge at that particular moment." Hunt glanced at Masters, who remained poker-faced. Vera went on: "You know, it seemed too good to be true at the time, so I actually made him wait until I'd had all night to think it over."

"Clever of me, don't you think?" asked Hunt, very pleased. "A wife in a working profession. She'll always be able to keep me if pharmaceutical advertising's axed."

Vera put her tongue out at Hunt and turned to leave. She stopped and said to Masters: "Keep it under your hat, won't you?"

"If you want me to, but why?"

171

Hunt said: "This firm won't employ husband and wife. In fact, that slob Torr—who I'm pleased to hear you've arrested for some dirty work or other—went so far as to get rid of one or other party if two people here announced they were engaged. We'd both rather keep our jobs together for as long as possible."

"I see. So it's a dark secret. I claim to be remarkably discreet."

Vera blew Hunt a kiss. He said: "See you for lunch, poppet. We'll go to The Pantiles for beer and a sandwich."

"Half twelve in the foyer," said Vera, and left.

Masters said: "You'd probably prefer to sit alone and daydream, but I want your attention for a few minutes."

"Shoot."

"When you promote a drug, what exactly happens?"

"New drug? Or an already established one?"

"Established."

They sat down. Hunt put his feet up on the desk.

"There's always a careful plan. It's based on past profits and what Market Research says the future potential is. If it's a real money-spinner we keep at it almost without stopping. But if it's just a good product which jogs along nicely on its own, we'll probably ignore it for a bit to give ourselves the chance of getting new numbers off the ground. After that, it may be considered worthwhile to spend quite a few thousands on it. What we would most likely try to do is boost sales to a new high level and then leave it there to jog along on its own again until the next time. You see, we've got so many products that we can't push them all at the same time, so we have to do this leapfrogging with the good, solid, routinely prescribed numbers."

"How do you go about giving this push to an established product?"

"With what we call a reminder campaign. This means

172

we don't start from scratch with nothing but solid, sober facts. The doctors know the drug already, so we can use a bit of impact in the ads. Our main idea is to recall the bull points of the product to their minds."

"Where do the advertisements appear?"

"Medical journals, mailings through the post. That sort of thing."

"Then what? Do you offer samples? Or send samples? Or do you wait for doctors to write in and ask for samples?"

"We offer samples, usually. But we call them clinical or professional supplies. We must preserve our ethical image."

"How do you make the offer?"

"We enclose a pre-paid postcard already printed with the offer. If it's not a scheduled drug all the doctor has to do is print his name and address and send it back to us. If it is a scheduled drug, we've got to have his signature on the card as well."

"Who gets the replies? Reculver?"

"Yes. He sends out the samples."

"Thanks. Now to be more specific. When did you last offer phenobarbitone?"

"Aha!" Hunt got to his feet with a bound. "Now I can see where the bloodhound's nose is pointing."

Masters said quietly: "And my questions are as secret and confidential as your engagement."

Hunt got the point. He opened the drawer of a filing cabinet. "We don't promote phenobarb in quite the same way as other things. It's so well known that all we have to do every once in a while is send a letter offering doctors a free supply for their night bags." He took out the Guard Book. On each page was the final copy of an advertisement with details of dates when it was sent out, and to whom. The last page held a letter and pre-paid postcard.

"Sent to all G.P.s on the thirtieth of September," he said. "We timed it then to catch them just as they'd settled down after their holidays. Just in time for a long hard winter. It's the only time of the year they're reputed to clean out and replenish night bags, so we should have got a good response."

Masters was looking at the postcard. "You offered them a choice of strengths. Very generous."

"It pays," said Hunt. "Believe you me, it pays, or we wouldn't do it."

"What about Nutidal?"

"Heaven help us," said Hunt. "We never stop with Nutidal. Look at this, this, and this." He held out several work bags and copy scamps. "All these on Nutidal for the next fortnight alone."

Masters said: "We'll skip Nutidal, then."

"I should if I were you. A.A. couldn't have checked out from an overdose of Nutidal. It wouldn't hurt a fly. Stick to phenobarb. That'll see anybody off, given enough."

"Thanks for the advice."

"Tit for tat. How're you getting on?"

"Progressing."

Hunt said: "When asked, the Chief Inspector was noncommittal. O.K. I understand."

Masters left him, having once more sworn to keep the engagement a secret. He made his way to Pharmacy.

Christine Blake had temporarily taken over Dieppe's office. She grinned self-consciously when Masters went in. She asked: "How's Teddy?"

"Reports are good. You won't have that chair for much longer, young lady."

She said: "If all you've come for is to gloat..."

"I want your opinion, as a pharmacist, of the standard of medical knowledge among typists in Barugt House.

Dr Mouncer told me some of them could give points to a doctor. Can I believe him?"

"You'd be a fool if you did. He must have been gassing."

"He was being a bit explosive. But I'd like your opinion, just the same."

"Some of the girls get a superficial knowledge about our own range of drugs, but we often forget how limited a single company is. Even so, the 'some' I'm talking about is mighty few. What you've got to remember is that we literally live with our own product names and so they, and the illnesses they're used for, are always in front of a typist. But to get any real medical knowledge, the girls would have to read and understand what they're copying, and very few of them even bother about the sense of what they're typing. Their mistakes prove it."

"Say one or two of them were in the habit of reading their copy. What then?"

"They'd have to have enough intelligence to understand it, a good enough memory to store it, and staying power to stick here long enough to accumulate a fund of knowledge and to let familiarity with medical terms play its part."

Masters said: "And you don't think many of them fulfil all these requirements?"

"Very few. And of those, only the girls who work in departments dealing with medical matters. Typists in Finance, Publicity, Admin and so on just don't get the chance to gain any medical knowledge."

Masters wasn't satisfied. It was too important. He said: "You've only given me the negative view."

"Is there any other?"

"If a really intelligent typist were to work in a medical department—say this one, for instance—for two or three years, and at the end of that time she had no medical or pharmaceutical knowledge, what then?"

Christine said: "I shouldn't agree she was intelligent. Given the intelligence, you simply can't help learning something, or at least getting a good enough basis for working up a knowledge should the need arise. It's the same with everything. Go as a typist to an Estate Agent and if you're not dumb you soon get to know what 'two stroke three bedrooms' means."

"Thank you. You've been most helpful, as you always are."

"You're a funny man for a detective. Not like your three mates who go around searching for things. You just potter about asking disconnected questions. I can't see how that helps you find murderers."

"Can't you? Well, in that case, you'll have no difficulty in forgetting everything I've asked, will you? Don't speculate, there's a good girl. Goodbye."

Masters went to the lifts. He intended to look for Green, but on the eighth floor Diane Murdo got in.

"You're a long way up," he said. She looked cuddly. He found himself thinking it was surprising there weren't more incidents in self-operating lifts. The proximity was so tempting.

She smiled: "I'm investigating a complaint."

"Food poisoning?"

"No. Nothing serious. Some silly weans have said that when the lifts stop on the first floor they suck in great gobs of smell from the kitchens and then carry them up and let them out on all the other floors. It's particularly bad if we're frying onions, they say. We're frying them today, so I came out to see what all the blather was about."

"Anybody who dislikes fried onions is soft in the head," said Masters. "Oh, blast. I didn't press my button."

"Never mind. We're at the first floor now. Have you had your coffee?"

176

"Not yet. I've been wandering round and haven't met the trolley." He'd made up his mind to accept the invitation before it was given. At her suggestion he followed her to her own little office sandwiched—opposite the dry goods pantry—betweeen the kitchen and the directors' dining-room. He was interested to see how she lived. The desk was a broad shelf under the window. There were a few box files, but her invoices hung in large bulldog clips from hooks on the walls. A menu for the month was pinned on a notice board.

As he followed her in he smelt the aroma of freshly percolated coffee. An electric percolator was plopping away on a tin tray carrying a Bass advertisement. She closed the two hatches leading to kitchen and directors' dining-room. With the door shut there was no more room than in the lift.

"Do you always make your own?" he asked.

She laughed. "I'd no more drink the stuff we send round in urns than the dishwater." She poured a large cup for him—a big, man-sized breakfast cupful, just muddied with top of the milk. His first sip of the scalding liquid made her point. She smiled her thanks at his appreciation. "Sit you down." She made him take the only chair. She perched herself on the desk shelf, holding her saucer high up in her left hand and the cup—from which she took quick little sips—in the other. He liked what he saw. He had a good view of her legs and a hint of thigh. He thought he wouldn't mind having this girl running a house for him. Both in practical ability and looks she'd got the makings of a wife any man would like.

"Do you manage to get up to Edinburgh often?" he asked.

She shook her head. The red hair swirled heavily. "Too expensive."

"Where do you live? In London?"

Again she shook her head and said: "Too expensive."
She put the cup and saucer down. "I share a flat in
Brendan's Wood with another girl. It's just a fourpenny
bus ride away. It's nice and quite reasonable, which I
like because I'm saving up to get married."

"Who to?"

"Phil Carr. He doesn't work here. He's in insurance.
I don't think I could tell you exactly what he does, but
I know he's going to get us a jolly good mortgage through
his work."

"Lucky you! No, thank you, I'll not drain the pot. I've
got some work to do."

She jumped down. "So've I. Don't be late for lunch.
I've made Scotch broth for you. D'you like that?"

"If you made it, I'm sure it'll be wonderful. By the
way, there's just one personal question."

"Yes?" She reddened, giving him the impression she
knew what he was going to ask.

"What was the trouble between you and Mr Huth?
And please don't say it was nothing. You got agitated
when I mentioned it the last time."

"Well it *was* nothing, really. He invited me out to
dinner and a theatre soon after I came here."

"You went?"

"Who wouldn't? He said his wife couldn't make it at
the last minute and it seemed a pity to cancel the ar-
rangements."

"You enjoyed yourself?"

"Very much. I was flattered. I was new here and the
chairman was taking me out. The trouble was...he
expected to be paid back afterwards."

"In kind?"

She nodded and began to turn over some bills, not
looking at him. She said quietly: "It had been marvellous up to then. He asked me if I had to get home

178

quickly. Of course I said I hadn't, because I expected him to say we'd go on to a night club and I'd never been to one and wanted to. Instead he said he knew a place that would let us have a room for a couple of hours." She turned to face him. "I'm not a Scot for nothing, you know. I told him straight there was going to be no peely wally with me. Then I left him and came home by train."

"How did he take it?"

"He couldn't do anything else but like it."

"And he never referred to it again?"

"I told you. He hardly said a word to me after that. At first I thought about getting another job, but then I met Phil so I wanted to stay in the district. Now I expect I'll stay here until after I'm married."

He said: "Thank you. Now I really will be on my way."

He found Green and the sergeants in Huth's office.

"It's no good," said Green. "We came up to tell you, and found the coffee here, so we waited to tell you. There's not a trace of any phenobarb going missing. Dieppe may be a bit of a dope himself, but he's got the system of accounting for scheduled drugs buttoned up tight. There's a signature to support every flaming tablet that's been sent out, and the balance is correct right down to the last grain."

Masters sat down and filled his pipe. He said: "We'll go over Reculver's books again."

"I tell you there's a reply paid card with a signature to support every sample sent out."

"I'm sure there is. Tell me how you checked them."

"There were over five thousand samples sent out in the last handout in September. We've checked every name on the signed cards with the names in the drug register that Reculver keeps for whatever official it is that comes to inspect them. Now *you* want to go over

179

them again! What's the matter with you? Think we can't read?"

Masters said: "For God's sake keep your shirt on. You're the one that's slipped up, aren't you?"

"No."

"Failed to find what I wanted, then. Now I've got another idea, and we're going to try it. If I'm right about this, we'll be nearly home. And you can stop looking so bolshie, because I think you've done what you did well enough, but I reckon the almighty Reculver's made a bloomer."

Green's face almost broke into a smile of pleasure. "No!" he said. "No! Not Reculver. That bastard's been dinning it into me for the past two days that it would be impossible for anybody to find a mistake in his books. And you should have seen the look on his face when I had to come away without catching him out. By heaven I hope you're right and we can nail him this time."

"Come on, then. We'll try it."

Reculver said to Masters: "I didn't think you'd find anything. Not in my department. We check and double check. Right to the last card and sample pack, that's us. We pride ourselves on being the most efficient department in the Company."

This was Masters' first meeting with Reculver. What he knew of him had come from Green's reports. And Masters didn't always trust Green's reports. In this case, as an example, he had thought Green had been laying it on with a trowel. Now he wasn't so sure. Reculver was giving him the V.I.P. treatment in a lordly manner. It made Masters squirm. He'd already envisaged Reculver as an old blowhard. Now he knew he was.

Masters said: "I'd like to talk about the pre-paid request cards for phenobarbitone clinical supplies."

"Your men have already checked them and found them correct in every detail."

Masters didn't like "your men." Neither did Green.

Masters said: "Inspector Green has so far only been making sure that requests, samples sent out and remaining stocks balance out. They do. Now we're going to do a further check. The real one. The other was only a preliminary. We're pretty efficient, too, you know."

Reculver blew out his cheeks. "A real check? What d'you mean? What other check can you do?"

"To begin with, you can tell me what precautions you take to ensure that the samples you send out do, in fact, go to bona fide doctors."

"That's easy. The cards are only sent to doctors in the first place, so they can only come back from doctors."

"But supposing a card should fall into the hands of somebody other than the intended recipient. This person signs it and sends it back. How do you guard against fraud of that sort?"

Reculver's jowls sank and he stared stupidly at Masters. Green, who could now recognize the pitfall grinned sourly. He said: "There's secretaries and cleaning women in surgeries. Dustbin men who collect the cards that are thrown out. Scores of unauthorized people could send those cards back and get free samples from you."

Reculver said: "Nobody can prevent fraud. We can't check up."

Masters said: "But you can. I've seen Medical Registers and Medical Directories in every office in Barugt House. You can check the names against those."

"But... there's over five thousand requests..."

"Can you guarantee that you haven't been guilty of sending scheduled drugs to unauthorized persons?"

Reculver turned pale. He stumbled to the door and shouted to the nearest typist: "Tell Mr Thomas I want him. And be quick about." He came slowly back to the chair. Before he could sit down there was a knock and a thin-faced young man came in. He paused when he saw the visitors.

"Sylvia said you wanted to see me urgently, Mr Reculver."

"Yes I do. You're in charge of sample requests. Do you check every request card against the Medical Directory when it's for a scheduled drug?"

"Hardly," said Thomas. "With one girl to help me? It'd take a month to do an average mailing."

"Get out," snapped Reculver.

Masters said: "Don't get annoyed with him. You're the boss."

Reculver snarled: "Blasted inefficiency. Incompetence in my own department. I won't have it. I'll be a laughing stock. Thomas will be out next week."

Masters got to his feet. "Leave him alone, or prove to me you gave him orders to carry out that check. Now, I want him and his assistant to help Inspector Green and my two sergeants." He turned to Green. "Put the five thousand cards in alphabetical order first and then do the check. I want every card that doesn't exactly match an entry in the Register or Directory."

"They won't do that," said Reculver in a surly voice. "Those books are out of date before they're printed. What with deaths and changes of address and so on. I tell you it's impossible to check."

Masters ignored him. He said to Green: "Even if they're as much as fifteen per cent out of date, which I doubt, there should only be about seven hundred to check more closely. They can be compared with the Company mailing list which must be almost up to date. That'll cut the job down to size."

Masters left Green to get on with it. He made his way back to Hunt's office. Hunt said: "What, you again? I'll be thinking you really do suspect me of killing A.A.

if I see much more of you." He minced across the room, aping a pansy. "People are beginning to notice, ducky."

"Two things," said Masters. "Who's recently been promoted in Research and Development?"

Hunt said: "Pal Joey. Joe March. Promoted a few months ago from Departmental Manager to Controller. A fiery character. He'll bite your head off."

"I'll take care. Now, second point. How many of those request cards do you print?"

"For a blanket mailing, like with phenobarb?"

Masters nodded.

"I don't know exactly, but there's roughly twenty-three thousand G.P.s who get one each and then there's the special list of about a couple of hundred, and we print a few over as a safety margin. I'd say about twenty-three and a half thou. But I can get you the exact figures from Publicity Admin if you like."

"Don't bother. What's this special list you mentioned?"

"Oh, that! We have to keep everybody informed of what we're sending out. If a rep bowls into a doctor's surgery and the doctor says, 'About this sample offer your firm's making...', it looks bad if the rep has to say, 'What sample offer?' D'you see what I mean? So we send all the reps a copy of everything we do. And the Directors and Heads of Departments. The reps' copies go in their weekly post. The others are just sent round the offices by hand, exactly as the doctors receive them. It's easier than writing a weekly information letter to keep everybody informed."

Masters' next visit was to Research and Development on the sixth floor. March, the Control Manager, was big, rawboned and ginger-haired. His high cheekbones stood out so that the cheeks themselves looked hollow and unhealthy. But March gave the impression of having great strength. He was the first senior member of Barugt management that Masters had seen badly dressed. He wore a bluish tweed suit that needed cleaning and pressing. His turn-down collar was wrinkled at the corners and there was a small burn hole in the front of his shirt. Masters thought he looked like a provincial reporter out of a job.

March said: "I've heard you've been ferreting about. Now it's my turn, is it? You'll be sucking a dry tit here. I know nothing about any murder—if it was murder, which I doubt."

"It definitely was murder. Take my word for it. As to whether you have any information about it, I'll be the judge of that. Just at the moment I want to know what your department does. What its function is."

"Mostly paper research."

"That doesn't mean much to me."

"I thought it wouldn't. D'you know what bench research is?"

"Laboratory work?"

"Practical investigation. This department spends most of its time on theoretical research. We work out on paper what should happen if certain experimentation is done. It sounds simple, but it's dam' technical and difficult."

"Do you ever touch chemicals?"

"Sometimes. We don't spend much of our time handling them, but the development side of our work is devoted to improving existing drugs. In connection with that all sorts of odd jobs crop up which you wouldn't understand."

"Try me."

"I'll give you a simple example that even a layman might understand. Have you ever heard of a giving bottle?"

"The one that hangs upside down on the stand when a transfusion's given?"

"So you do know something. Not only for transfusions. For drips and all intravenous administration bigger than a syringe will take. If we produce a drug that has to be administered that way, I'm reponsible for finding the best type of giving set. Right size bottle, right harness, right needle, right tube, right material that won't react with the drug, and so on. We check them all here. In a case like that we'd handle both empty sets and full sets, so you can say we'd actually be handling the drug itself."

Masters said: "I'm with you so far. Go on."

March glared. "What for?"

"I want to know."

"I'll still try and keep it simple. If we've got an established drug with an excipient of a certain type of starch or sugar or what-have-you ... you know what I'm talking about?"

"Excipient? Yes. I should say base, myself, but then I'm only a layman."

"Smart, eh? Well, suppose—and this is always happening in this benighted country today—suppose the supplier of that particular excipient were suddenly to tell us he's not going to make any more because it's not an economic proposition, I'd have to find an alternative with the same inert properties and a make-up that wouldn't affect the performance of the active ingredients. So we'd be handling those chemicals, too."

"In that case, I'd be right in supposing that over a period of a year or two you would handle liquids and solids, break down tablets, fill capsules, weigh powders, mix ointments and so on?"

"All that and more."

"Your staff would help?"

March said: "What the hell d'you think I keep them for? They're not usually all that pretty to look at."

"Don't be offensive," said Masters. "I may be taking

up some of *your* valuable time, but I'm not wasting my own, which is more important."

"Asking footling questions?"

"I often do. I daresay some of your paper research turns out to be a bit footling at times."

"Time spent in research is never wasted."

"That's my point. But all research isn't immediately productive."

March said: "Ninety per cent of research results in very little. But it all adds to total knowledge."

"Just like my investigations. Now, to get back to cases. Does everybody who works for you get to know something about drugs and how to handle them?"

"Everybody? Yes, they certainly do. If they don't know how when they arrive they soon have to get stuck in. I wouldn't keep anybody who didn't."

"And your typists?"

"Them too. There's not all that much typing in this department. We don't send out letters and all that tosh. Only reports, and they're not all that frequent. So the typists have to do the non-technical jobs. Use balances and mixers. That sort of thing. If they're frightened of getting their nail varnish chipped I sling 'em out."

Masters got up. "Thank you. That's all I wanted to know for the moment. But I expect to be back. Probably after lunch."

"Hell," said March. "No wonder crime's on the increase."

Green was enjoying himself. "It's going to be a hell of a job, but it's going to be worth it. I know we're on the right track this time. So do the others. They're working like Mary making duff." He rubbed his hands together. "You wouldn't like to guess in which half of the alphabet we ought to start looking, would you?"

Masters said: "No, I wouldn't. Nor which quarter either. It's got to be done so that there's no chance of a slip-up. How far have you got?"

"We've done two or three hundred." He held up a few discards. "When there's enough of these I'm going down to check them with the mailing list personally."

Masters said: "Do that. They're the important ones. I'll see you at lunchtime." He went into Reculver's office. The manager had settled down to work, but he didn't appear to be giving it much attention. There was fear in his eyes when he looked up and saw Masters.

"Have you ... have you found anything?"

"Not yet. Now I want the internal indents for the non-scheduled drugs."

Reculver said: "There won't be many. The shop supplies the personal needs of everybody below the rank of departmental manager. We only supply top management because we don't expect them to go and stand in the shop queue. We also meet indents from Pharmacy, Publicity and Research and Development, but the amounts they need, in comparison, are quite small."

"Show me."

Reculver called for the indents. A typist brought them in. For ten minutes Masters thumbed through them. He found what he was looking for. He impounded the whole bundle of indents.

"I'm taking these. Would you like a receipt?"

Reculver said: "It doesn't matter. Do you mean to say that some member of top management murdered A.A.?" Masters thought that Reculver was just the type to hold an outsize opinion of everybody higher up the ladder than himself. The Reculvers of his experience always held tenaciously to the belief that only the lesser lights commit crime.

Masters snapped: "What do you expect? That some

little fifteen-year-old messenger girl murdered him?"

"No, of course not."

"Then you shouldn't be surprised. And keep quiet about these indents."

Masters called on Barraclough to ask him some questions about the indents. After a satisfactory five minutes he returned to Huth's office and helped himself to a large gin and tonic from the corner wine cupboard. He was sitting thinking when Green appeared, ready to go to lunch.

"How much longer will you be with those cards?"

"About an hour."

"Slip along, then. I want the answer quick."

Green said: "You're going to give us time to eat?"

"If you've got to."

At two o'clock Masters again called on March. March said: "What the devil do you want now? Incompetent bureaucrats popping in and out all day! It's getting beyond a joke."

Masters thought March was a bore and said so and continued: "So please keep quiet. I really haven't the time to listen to your outbursts."

March slumped back in his chair, his pale face curiously flushed with anger. He slammed the pencil he was holding onto the desk and asked: "What do you want?"

"I told you I'd be coming back. I want your opinion of Mr Huth."

"Do you? And I suppose you'll be surprised when I tell you he was a two-faced bastard."

"I am. He gave you a handsome promotion a month or two ago."

"I suppose you think I ought to go down on my knees

every time his name's mentioned. I'll tell you why he gave me my promotion—disregarding the fact that I had thoroughly earned it—it was to keep me quiet."

"Most of his other employees find him fair-minded."

"Of course they do. I was sucked in myself, for years. I thought he was a thrusting businessman, research-minded, and big enough to accept the advice his experts like me gave him. That's what we're here for."

"But he wasn't?"

"He didn't even try to utilize all the possibilities of this firm."

"I've had all that explained to me."

"Explained away, you mean. Chaps like me slog our guts out to give him products which will corner every market, and what does he do? He cold-shoulders the ideas. I've searched for marginal improvements on drugs, and found them. There's a good dozen of our products could be improved at no cost to ourselves, and they'd rake in the money. Would he listen? Not likely. Out of the increased business he could pay some of us a bit more to offset the rise in the cost of living, and do sick people a power of good at the same time. I take trouble to find out what doctors want and then I bust a gut trying to give it them. Three entirely new products have been suggested by this department in the past year. With all the relevant medical and marketing facts to show they were good propositions. And what has Huth done about them? Nothing."

"You're frustrated?"

"That's putting it mildly. I want to do things—in my profession and in my life. I want to help sick people but Huth has queered my pitch. I've wanted to get married but couldn't even think about it until Huth saw fit to pay me a bit more—not for my services, but to keep me quiet."

"Are you thinking of marrying shortly?"

"Since I was promoted I've become engaged; but for God's sake don't say anything to anybody about it. It's unofficial."

"I won't. Did you ever discuss these points with Mr Huth?"

"Are you serious? I could never get near him."

"But no doubt you've voiced your opinions pretty widely?"

March looked at him hard. "What are you getting at? I didn't do the old bastard in."

"I'm not suggesting you did."

"That's all right then. No. I've written a few pertinent memos, but I've kept my mouth shut in Barugt House. With creepers like Torr about it wasn't safe to speak your mind here."

"You needn't worry about Torr any longer."

"That's one good piece of work the police have done."

"You've had your say, though—probably to friends and acquaintances."

"To my fiancée only. She's the only one who'd listen. I say, you will keep quiet about her, won't you? She's a bloody fine girl. I don't know what the hell she sees in me, but I know what I see in her, so I don't want to spoil it all by jumping the gun."

Masters stood up. "Thank you, Mr March. I'll not tell anybody in Barugt House about your engagement." He left abruptly, without saying goodbye.

Green said: "We're just finishing off. There's twenty-seven cards we can't place."

Masters took them from him and studied them one by one. After several minutes he looked up and nodded to Green who grinned back in triumph. Masters said quietly: "Take a handful of the cards, just so they won't be able to check back on the one we want. Then give yourself a treat and tell Reculver he's made quite a lot of mistakes. I've one more short call to make, then I'll meet you in Huth's office."

Masters went down to the first floor and tapped on the door of Diane Murdo's tiny room.

"You decided you'd come for tea, too?"

"No. I want to ask you some questions." His tone warned her that this was no social visit. She backed slowly into the room as he closed the door behind him.

It took him less than five minutes to get her answers to his questions. He left Diane Murdo white-faced and incredulous. He didn't know how he felt himself, angry or sorry, but he jabbed the lift button viciously.

Green, Hill and Brant stood close together in Huth's office, not talking. Masters came in heavily. He said: "Ring Superintendent Bale. Tell him to send another car over straight away."

"With a warrant?" asked Green.

"Not just yet. Tell him we'll need one later tonight, but we'll have to have a session in his office first. Don't say any more than that, and hurry, please. I want us to be away from here before work stops, and they finish at four on Fridays."

Hill silently handed Masters a cup of tea. Nobody said anything until Green had finished phoning. Then Green said: "The Super's coming himself. He'll be here in ten minutes."

"Good. Pack up everything and get it into the car. When Superintendent Bale comes, Green, I want you and Brant to help him. Remember, it's just for questioning at the moment."

6

Masters was sitting in Bale's chair, with his back to the fire. The superintendent joined him. Bale said: "Do you want me here?"

Masters said: "I'd rather you weren't, but it's your case. Green will be here taking notes. Too many of us might make certain things more difficult."

Bale said: "I'll keep out of it." He left immediately.

The room was barely furnished. The desk was varnished yellow, the filing cabinets olive drab. The square of carpet, once dark red and patterned, was now an overall grey from overmuch use and the ingrained dust of years. Bale's few pictures were all framed photographs of former members of the force. Nowhere had he a splash of colour to relieve the monotony of the cream-washed walls. Even the curtains were gravy-coloured. The visitors' chairs were hard-seated, with spell backs. Masters felt depressed. He knew he shouldn't have been. He should have been happy at winding up a case so quickly and so successfully.

Green ushered her in and sat her down opposite Masters. Then he took a seat at a smaller table which the station sergeant had sent in specially for him.

Masters looked at her. She gazed back for a moment. Even though all desire for her had now left him, because the thought of it sickened him in these circumstances, he still thought her lovely. The violet eyes still mocked him. She said: "You look much younger than you did the last time I saw you."

He replied: "I feel older. You've put years on me." For a moment he wanted to reach out and slap her. Call her a silly little bitch! Drive home to her the enormity of her crime, which she seemed to be ignoring. Her eyes seemed to gloat, as if she could guess his thoughts, and found them cause for derision. Then she looked away, opened the handbag on her lap, took out a folded handkerchief and blew her nose gently. He could smell the perfume. Unobtrusive perfume. Probably some Huth had bought her.

He said: "You're not under arrest. You're here of your own free will for questioning. Do you understand?"

"All except the free will bit."

"Before I begin, do you want to ring a solicitor?"

"What for?"

"Please don't be flippant. I strongly suspect you of murdering Mr Huth. What we are about to discuss now, together with the evidence I already have, will determine what action Superintendent Bale takes after we've finished. If you feel you want legal advice, please say so, now. Inspector Green is recording the fact that I am making you this offer."

She said: "I don't think you can have any evidence against me, otherwise you'd have arrested me already."

Masters said: "For God's sake, woman!"

She turned to Green. "Do you know what evidence he has?"

Green said: "No, I don't. But I'm sure he's got it if he says he has. And he won't be trying to trap you."

She said: "Before I consent to answer your questions, I want to know what evidence it is you have against me."

"It's unusual, but look at these." Masters showed her a request card for phenobarbitone and an internal indent for non-scheduled drugs. "Will these satisfy you?"

She stared for a moment, without making any attempt to touch them where they lay on the desk turned towards her. He was watching her face. He imagined it lost a little colour. She looked up at him and said quietly: "It seems I'm in a bit of a mess."

"I think so, and I'm glad you've realized it for yourself. Shall we go ahead now?"

She nodded.

Two hours later, Green escorted her from the room. Masters stayed at the desk, writing, for another hour.

Dear Superintendent Bale,

When you called me in to investigate the death of Adam Huth, you said you would need a lot of convincing that his death was not murder. The official report will show that he died as the result of the wilful action of the person you now hold in custody, accused of murder. The case is yours, and I cannot suggest how you should interpret the evidence. But before the accused appears before the special sitting tomorrow morning, I should like you to read my account of the investigation and the conclusions I have come to.

I was faced with the problems of finding the killer of an able but kind and shy man. I had to accomplish two things. Find somebody who disliked him enough to kill him; and find some weakness in his character which would cause somebody not only to hope for his death, but actually to bring it about.

There was only one person—March—who admitted a dislike of Huth; and this dislike, though it had apparently genuine grounds, was based on a misunderstanding of policy instigated by Huth in the best interests of his workers. Even to March, Huth showed understanding and kindness by promoting him to a high position in the Company. There were two others who had grounds to hate Huth, although they never admitted to it. The first was the Company Pharmacist, who had just been dismissed—again, according to Huth's lights, in the best interests of the man. The second was Mrs Huth, who obviously recognized the inadequacy of her marriage, but who nevertheless insisted that her husband treated her with great understanding and kindness.

I encountered March very late on in the investigation, when I was virtually sure who the killer was. Even so, I considered him carefully, but his temperament convinced me that he would use his tongue to settle a quarrel rather than any other means. This conclusion was reinforced in my mind by the fact that March was a very efficient research chemist, unlikely to resort to using a very inefficient poison to polish off a victim. By this time I had realized that phenobarbitone, in the dosage I thought it was possible to administer to Huth, was not a sure killer. Miss Blake, the pharmacist, had made this quite clear some days before when she said that medical textbooks quoted examples of people surviving really massive doses of this drug. This evidence gave me one of my important leads. I believed the killer to be somebody with only a small, superficial knowledge of drugs and their activity.

Also, I excluded Dieppe, on the grounds that he was

too knowledgeable a pharmacist to use phenobarbitone. It was clear to me from the beginning that whoever killed Huth must have known the victim was currently taking a course of Nutidal treatment. I satisfied myself that Dieppe did not know this and, additionally, it appeared evident that Dieppe could never have brought himself into such close contact with Huth as the killer had need to do. I read Dieppe as the sort of man who, having been dismissed by Huth, would try to keep out of sight of his persecutor rather than encounter him.

Mrs Huth was always a possibility, with a big motive and, possibly, a hidden grievance. I bore her in mind throughout, but at no point did I find one tangible piece of evidence that suggested she had murdered her husband. My impression of her was of a candid, forthright woman whose integrity was apparent at both our interviews.

There were, of course, other possible suspects. Dr Mouncer knew Huth was taking Nutidal, but here again I would have expected a physician of Mouncer's calibre to use a more subtle, surer poison than phenobarbitone. There were no other grounds for suspicion other than the possible motive of stepping into Huth's shoes. My enquiries satisfied me that Mouncer knew he would not get the appointment, and that he would have refused it had it been offered to him.

Miss Krick, as you suggested, could also be considered as a suspect. But her ingenuous attitude, combined with a story that dovetailed reasonably no matter what tests I put it to, convinced me that this woman had neither the knowledge nor the temperament to murder her chief. I am, however, grateful to Miss Krick for her transparent simplicity. The fact that she had, from time to time, been seduced by Huth, gave me the first sign of a lead in the case.

Huth's character was apparently without blemish. But he had enjoyed the favours of his rather pathetic P.A. on half a dozen occasions, at times when a man in Huth's position, and with his apparent reputation, would have considered the girl to be under his protection, as an employee obliged by circumstances to attend conferences with him. It seemed strange to me that a man like Huth, with so much to lose by a scandal, should risk so much for so little, unless he were subject to an unconquerable urge. I appeared to be thinking along the right lines when I asked Miss Murdo if she had ever met Huth socially. The question embarrassed her to such an extent that I later questioned her closely as to the reason for this reaction. I learned that Huth had made an attempt to seduce her, too. It seemed fair to suppose that Huth's occasional lapses with Miss Krick and his attempt with Miss Murdo would not have satisfied him, and that I should, therefore, consider whether he had not a regular mistress.

If I was right, and Huth had an outsize libido, I had found the flaw in his character. Mrs Huth confirmed that she had never—not for want of trying—been able to satisfy her husband's sexual demands. She did not go as far as saying that her husband was a lustful man, but she did comment on the fact that though he was still virile, he made no excessive demands on her during the period of her change of life.

Up until that time, two years before his death, he and his wife had apparently managed to get along successfully, even with the marital difficulties of two unequally matched partners to frustrate them. I believe Huth did his damnedest to remain faithful to his wife until then, and as far as I know succeeded in doing so. Don't forget that he was a good man in all other respects, even though some of his kindnesses seemed to emerge more in his own favour than that of others. But when his wife approached the menopause and the situation changed for the worse from his point of view, he made his choice. He decided virtually to opt out of the marriage bed—out of kindness to his wife—and to allow his libido free rein elsewhere.

At this point I think I should say that I don't think Huth was a lecher. He had unrequited sexual desire, but I am doubtful if anybody other than his wife and mistresses knew it. Dr Mouncer told me that Huth even disliked dirty stories. I have made inquiries into the causes of libido. There are various theories, most of which suggest that those who suffer from it can be regarded as almost permanently under the influence of a self-produced aphrodisiac. The chemistry of their bodies is simply too androgenic: too many male hormones.

Having discovered the flaw in Huth's character, I needed to find a personable woman who could have been his permanent mistress. The girls in Barugt House are as pleasant looking—or as motley—as you could find anywhere. But I judged that Huth would look for personality and intelligence as well as physical beauty. I had two reasons for this supposition. His wife is an extremely intelligent woman, and men often go for the same type a second time. Miss Krick is, I should say, unintelligent, and this is why he had so little to do with her. Miss Murdo is attractive and intelligent, but she has been fully occupied in getting herself engaged and preparing for marriage to another man, and so I ruled her out. Miss Chambers, a different type again, but personable and intelligent. She confessed she had been fully occupied thinking how to bring Hunt, the copywriter, to his senses. The only other intelligent and attractive woman that came within the scope of my investigation was Joan Parker. I had to consider her, and almost immediately found grounds for suspicion. You now hold her on a charge of murder.

The case against Parker built up swiftly. I had to satisfy myself whether she had the opportunity to kill Huth. If so, how and why.

Parker made the mistake on my first day at Barugt House of telling me that Miss Krick had visited the secretariat for only five minutes, when Miss Krick herself had told me her stay had been twenty minutes. I was told Parker mistook the time because she, Parker, had gone into Barraclough's office after five minutes. Barraclough's office has two doors. One from the secretariat, and one from the vestibule. If Parker had carried a paper through to Barraclough, and then left immediately by the door into the vestibule, she could have entered Huth's office unnoticed, and had a quarter of an hour alone with him. So Parker had the opportunity, and despite careful enquiries, I could find no trace of any other visit made to Huth, except that of Dr Mouncer for his usual coffee break.

I questioned Miss Krick about status in Barugt House so that I could learn Parker's history with the firm. Parker had been a typist with Pharmacy and a secretary with Research and Development. I enquired from various sources whether she would gain any medical knowledge from this experience. I was told that an intelligent girl would pick up a superficial knowledge of drugs in Pharmacy, and learn how to handle them in Research and Development. Both these facts were vital in building up the case against Parker.

I still had no proof that Parker had been Huth's permanent mistress, but I was extremely surprised to find that so attractive a woman had avoided marriage, or even an engagement, by her middle twenties. And yet Parker obviously liked men. She was at ease with me, and treated Barraclough in such a way as to show she was a woman used to the company of men. Her conversation showed she spent much of her time with men. I felt sure there must be a man in her life and, in view of other things, felt certain it was Huth. If this was so, it is certain she would know Huth was taking Nutidal—an important point.

To bring the murder home to Parker I had to discover how it was done. We knew Huth had died from an overdose of phenobarbitone potentiated by alcohol. We started a thorough search for missing phenobarbitone, but the method of accounting is so thorough that we could find no discrepancy. However, I discovered that samples of phenobarbitone had recently been offered to doctors. Whether Parker, with her limited medical knowledge, had first of all decided to use phenobarbitone for her purpose, or whether she merely took it when the opportunity arose, I cannot say. But directors, among whom was her chief, Barraclough, had delivered to them, by hand, all sample offers sent out by publicity. A copy of the letter offering phenobarbitone, together with the prepaid request card for samples, was taken into the secretariat and handed to Parker, as his P.A., to hand on to Barraclough in the usual way. She didn't pass them on. She filled in the card with the name and qualifications of a real doctor, taken from the list, but added her own address. Here I had a slice of luck. When I saw the card, put aside because the address didn't agree with the one in the Medical Directory, I realized I had heard of that particular postal area for the first time earlier that day. Miss Murdo had told me that she was sharing a flat with a girl in Brendan's Wood. The card was addressed to Brendan's Wood. I saw Miss Murdo immediately and she told me Parker was her flat-mate. Miss Murdo will also testify that, unusually for her,

Parker got up early enough to meet the post on the two or three days during which the phenobarbitone tablets were being sent out.

The great mystery about this case as far as my team was concerned was the lack of tablet sediment in the brown drug bottle found on Huth's desk. It was clean. Hill did not appreciate that Nutidal is put up in capsules—little gelatine torpedoes which are obviously watertight and dustproof. The purpose of capsule coating is to delay the action of the drug until the stomach juices have dissolved the casing. They are known variously as sustained release capsules or timed disintegration capsules. It was obvious that if Huth was taking Nutidal, any drug he was given in place of it would have to have the appearance of Nutidal capsules. This suggested that the phenobarbitone he had taken had been concealed in capsules instead of Nutidal powder. I should have been surprised if there had been signs of phenobarbitone in the bottle. If this theory was correct, I had to prove that Parker had also got hold of some Nutidal tablets.

Although Nutidal is not a Dangerous Drug within the meaning of the Acts, no pharmacist will sell it without a prescription. Nor would the Barugt Company shop. However, because it is not scheduled, it is much easier to obtain in Barugt House than phenobarbitone. Parker's scheme was simple. On the Friday afternoon before Huth's death she went into Barraclough and said she had a headache, but was too late to go to the Company shop, which only opens at lunchtimes. As he was fully entitled to do, Barraclough agreed to write an internal indent on Reculver's department for some mild analgesic for Parker and for some antacid tablets which he suddenly remembered his wife wanted. Parker typed these items on the indent. Barraclough signed it. Parker then returned to her own office and added, above the signature, another item—a bottle of Nutidal capsules. She went down to Reculver's department herself to collect the drugs, so by Friday evening she had both phenobarbitone and Nutidal—the means she needed for carrying out her plan.

Although it is unnecessary to prove one, I find that the discovery of the motive is the greatest help an investigator can have in a case such as this. Unfortunately discovery is often difficult, and in this case I had to rely on theories. There were many of these, but what finally put me on the right track was a request from Hunt and Vera Chambers. They asked me to keep the news of their engagement secret because Barugt would not continue to employ both parties to an engagement or marriage. Why this is so, I can't think, but I understand it is a common practice with many employers, including the Government. When I saw March, he told me he had been engaged for a short time. There was no reason why he should tell me the name of his fiancée, and I didn't ask for it. But he also made a point of asking me to keep the information to myself. To me, this was a clear indication that his future wife must also be an employee at Barugt. Now March is not the sort of chap to suffer fools gladly, and I couldn't see him tying himself to some hare-brained little typist. He, like Huth, would be interested only in an intelligent woman. And yet he told me that his fiancée was a beautiful girl. Naturally, as I had Parker very much in mind at this time, I immediately thought of her. If I was right, lots of things would become clearer. I would now have the situation where Parker was the mistress of the man her future husband hated. An ideal situation for incubating murder.

Miss Murdo was again useful to me. I wondered how

Parker had managed to keep her flat-mate in ignorance of the fact that she was Huth's mistress. Strangely enough, she managed it by the simple trick of making no secret of the fact that she was running around with a married man named Leslie. Leslie is Huth's second Christian name. Parker never took Leslie to the flat because Miss Murdo, being a bit of a "Wee Free," would certainly have objected. That was her excuse for preserving Huth's mystery. Murdo told me, however, that though she didn't know March and Parker were actually engaged, she did know they'd been seeing something of each other recently. A fact which pleased Miss Murdo, who hated seeing Parker throw herself away on a married man.

This was as far as I could go. From then on, everything on my part was conjecture, based on what I knew. When I questioned Parker tonight she realized that as I knew so much, but not all, her own account of what happened would probably sound better than mine. Here is the gist of what she told me.

Just as Huth had attempted to seduce Murdo, so with Parker. Only this time he was successful. Parker admitted that her salary as a newly promoted P.A. wouldn't run to paying for half a modern flat and buying all the nice things a girl like her thrives on and dreams about. Huth was her opportunity to get them. More than that, she said he promised her marriage after divorce from his present wife. I can believe this. Parker is the type of girl any man would like to marry, and when he was in her arms I can understand Huth promising her the moon.

But he was too clever a businessman to put his promises into practice. Why should he divorce a wife he wanted to keep when he could have Parker on the side? And would a big American corporation, selling ethical drugs, like the idea of scandal within its ranks? Whatever the reason, Huth made no attempt to fulfill his promises, and Parker eventually realized he had no intention of doing so. By then she was becoming disenchanted. She wanted a home and family—in marriage—which she considers is the right of every woman. And in the case of a woman as beautiful as this, I agree with her, if that is what she wants. It was about this time that Parker became friendly with March again. I think she was caught on the rebound because she had previously worked for March—before she teamed up with Huth—and though March had shown a great interest in her then, she had not responded as fully as he would have liked. According to Parker, March pestered her in those days, and she had occasionally gone out with him, but his dourness offended her. But it appears that after March got his promotion he felt he was in a position to offer Parker everything a girl could want, so he had then set his cap at her in earnest. March the Control Manager was a new person, and this time Parker had not sent him packing. She said she had found a surprising lot to like in the man. I got the impression that she is very much in love with him, and her subsequent actions seem to bear this out.

When March proposed marriage, Parker accepted gladly. But by now she realized that March had a pathological hatred of Huth. She was in a fix, but she told Huth she was ending their relationship, praying that it could end without fuss, and that March would never get to hear of it. She said she feared that if March did learn she had been Huth's mistress he would certainly throw her over and probably kill Huth. She insists that she really did fear that March would attack Huth, and having met March, I am inclined to agree with her that that is just the impression he gives one—or tries to.

But Huth wouldn't play ball. I imagine he thought

that a man of his age would never again be able to get himself a permanent mistress as attractive as Parker, and so he refused to let her go. He knew she was a necessity to him. At first he made no threats. He simply refused to accept the situation, and when a man in his position, with a forceful personality, takes that stand, it is difficult for a young woman employee—even though she is his mistress—to counter him effectively. Parker, however, was adamant, and there was a row, during which Parker inadvertently let slip the fact that the man she intended to marry was the newly-promoted March. She soon realized the magnitude of her mistake. Huth said he would inform March if—and she quoted—"the nonsense went any further." As you may expect, this attitude of Huth's only made Parker more determined to leave him and marry March. But the situation she had most feared had arisen. She really believed March would go berserk; and what made it worse in her eyes was the fact that Huth, not realizing just how much March hated him, would carry out his threat. She came to the conclusion that to stop Huth ruining her life further, and to stop her future husband committing murder, she would have to give Huth a serious jolt. That is when the idea of really frightening Huth entered her mind. And that, she claims, is what she set out to do. Not to murder him. Her idea was to make him so ill that it would bring him to his senses when he was told how it had happened. If he were to make an official fuss about being doped, he couldn't have hoped to keep the reason for it quiet; or if he were to accuse her privately of trying to kill him she had intended to say that March knew all about their relationship and that it was he who had concocted the plan as a warning against further blackmail. She hoped this would deter him from ever mentioning the subject to March.

It was a crazy scheme, but I believe the girl was desperate in the face of Huth's blackmail. And I think she was right not to imagine Huth would eventually relent. He wouldn't relent over dismissing Dieppe, in spite of pleas by Dr Mouncer, and this case affected him much more personally than did Dieppe's future. A man with his urge could never give up. Parker probably sensed that better than anybody. So she took steps to get hold of the phenobarbitone. She says that at the time she had no definite idea how she would use it, but she had some nebulous plan of dropping the tablets in his drinks, when they were together. She was still consorting with him, because he would accept nothing less, and she knew she had to string him along until such time as she could put some plan into action. That is how and when she got to know he was taking Nutidal.

This is where Huth's Victorian attitude helped her. He didn't take the Nutidal bottle home. He didn't want his wife to see it. He took the capsules in his office, except at the weekend, when he managed to take them in private. He was able to be lax with the timing of the doses because though the instructions say "two capsules four times daily," it doesn't matter much whether the intervals are exactly spaced or not. It is the amount of Nutidal that is taken in seven days that really matters, and from what Dr Mouncer told me, it should be possible to take four capsules twice daily without causing harm. Huth must have been aware of this, and in order to cut down the number of doses, he followed this alternative course. Parker learned what he was doing, and knowing what the recommended full course of treatment was, she was able to calculate that he would have just four left to take on Monday.

During the weekend she opened and emptied a number of Nutidal capsules, ground the phenobarbitone tab-

lets to powder and refilled the capsules. She knew how
to do this well enough as a result of her work in Research and Development. The capsules are made in two
halves: two little thimbles which join in the middle.
Gentle heat only is required to separate the two halves
and reseal them, and as Parker had fifty-six to play
with, a few discards wouldn't matter.

Nutidal capsules hold half a gramme of powder. The
large tablets of phenobarbitone contain one grain of
pure drug, and each tablet weighs one-eighth of a
gramme. Each refilled Nutidal capsule would, therefore, hold four grains of pure phenobarbitone. The maximum therapeutic dose is ten grains in twenty-four
hours, and even these produce unpleasant side effects.
As I have said earlier, the exact lethal dose differs from
person to person, but it is certain that sixteen grains
taken all at once would cause anybody the serious trouble that Parker says she hoped to induce in Huth.

Her plan of action was simple. It all depended on
being able to see Huth on Monday morning before he
took his Nutidal. She had planned to call on him as if
sent by Barraclough. As it turned out, Krick left her
office and seemed likely to be away for some time, so
Parker seized that opportunity. Her excuse to Huth
himself was to announce to him that she had taken a
step he had long urged her to take: stopped smoking
cigarettes. It was a poor excuse, but she could think of
no other, and because she wished to distract his attention while she was with him, she thought of announcing
at the same time that she had taken to smoking one of
the brands of mild cigars recommended for women. She
would then offer him one. To make sure he took it—
she was well aware of his reluctance to smoke any brand
but his own—she set out to be particularly pleasant to
him. Huth didn't carry a cutter, because the cigars he

smoked were ready cut, but she knew he kept a cutter in his top left-hand drawer, which was also where he kept his bottle of Nutidal.

I imagine that Parker could charm the birds from the trees. Certainly she could get an immediate response from a man with Huth's urges. So she had little difficulty in getting a happy and grateful Huth to accept a cigar. It was she who opened the drawer for the cutter and pointed out that he hadn't finished the Nutidal. While Huth was busy with the cigar, the real Nutidal bottle went into the left-hand pannier pocket of her skirt, and the bogus bottle, taken from the same pocket, was put on the desk. Huth took his four capsules obediently, and chose sherry to wash them down with. While he was getting the sherry from the pedestal cupboard, Parker gave the Nutidal bottle a flick with her handkerchief. It needed very little wiping because she had cleaned it well before going to his office. At some time after that Huth must have picked up the bottle, because we found one set of his prints on it. Parker left him, saying she wanted to be away before Krick returned. The whole episode had taken probably less than five minutes. Parker returned to Barraclough's office as if returning from the lavatory.

Mouncer thought Huth looked peaky at coffee time, but not so seriously as to cause him to take any action. The capsules had probably only just begun to disintegrate by then, but by lunchtime Huth was really beginning to feel the effects. The bad taste in his mouth was not caused by Parker's cigar, but by the metallic taste of too much phenobarbitone. He took a fair amount of sherry and brandy in an attempt to brighten himself up. This was the worst thing he could have done. He went upstairs to his office, but by this time he felt so ill that he locked the door and sat down. He didn't want

Krick or anybody else to see him in that state, and no doubt he hoped the malaise would pass off in a few minutes. I imagine it was then, while he was still in possession of his faculties, that he helped himself to more brandy. Soon after that he must have been asleep, in a coma, or had become so weak that he was unable to help himself. Krick didn't enter the office, nor did Mrs Pallot, until next morning.

That is how Huth died. In giving you the full story and finding the murderess I have done what you asked me to do. While it may seem a good job done to you, I am far from satisfied. I personally believe that this was not intended as murder, and had it not been for Huth's large intake of alcohol, I think he would still be alive. Parker will be able to claim this, and she will get away with it when the jury learns she was being blackmailed. The defence will undoubtedly plead extenuating circumstances because of the blackmail, and they'll also say there was no intention to kill. They will make a good point of this because of the inefficiency of phenobarbitone as a poison, and Parker's appearance in court will help them. I feel that if you insist on a charge of murder you will not make it stick. With manslaughter, you will get a verdict.

I have written this in a private letter because you will realize it cannot be included in an official report. But I feel I owe you the benefit of my knowledge over what the charge preferred should be. However, as I pointed out earlier, I cannot instruct you on how to interpret evidence. My job is merely to provide you with it to use as you think best.

George.

Bale read the letter through twice and then called for his station sergeant.

"Is Chief Inspector Masters still in the station?"

"He was going out when he handed me the letter, sir. For supper. I directed him and Inspector Green to that little Italian place."

"The Pantellaria?"

"That's it, sir."

"I'll join them."

"They said they'd be back, sir."

"Did they? What for?"

"To see a chap who's been making a nuisance of himself outside, sir. His name's March. It seems he knows the girl you've arrested, and he wants to know what's going on. Chief Inspector Masters left his two sergeants to deal with him and said he'd come back to explain after he'd had his meal."

Bale sat and waited. Masters' interview with Parker had started at five and lasted over two hours, and the writing of the letter had taken another hour. It was after nine o'clock when the two of them returned.

Bale said: "I've read your letter."

Masters didn't reply. Bale went on: "The decision won't be mine. It'll be up to the C.C., or even the Director. You've got to remember the inquest finding."

"I've remembered all these. I just don't think you'll get the charge to stick."

"Maybe not, but before I do anything about it I want to know where your personal feelings are in this."

"Mine? They're involved all right."

"I thought so."

"I don't like sending a young girl to jail for life to pay for one mistake, made when she was at her wits' end."

"So?"

"That's all."

Bale looked at him carefully for a moment. He said: "You don't give me much choice, do you?"

Masters said: "Or myself."

Green said impatiently: "What the hell is this? I don't get it."

Bale turned to him. "If you don't mind my saying so, Inspector Green, you're not a very perspicacious officer. Masters has suggested that Parker should be charged with manslaughter, not murder."

"They can alter the charge in court, can't they?"

"It's better if it doesn't come to that. My worry is that Masters is the prosecution's key witness. What he's as good as said is that if we insist on a charge of murder he'll do everything he can—in the box or out of it—to get the case dismissed. If we agree to manslaughter he'll go along with us."

"So what?"

"If he were to do that it would be curtains for him at the Yard. If he had to adopt that attitude it would leave him with no choice but to resign."

Green said: "Do you mean to tell me, Superintendent, that you don't know the code of the force better than that? If an officer believes that a person charged with murder is not guilty of the crime, it is his duty to say so. In fact he would be in the wrong if he didn't fight for justice. Why should our friend here resign if he believes the girl innocent, and goes to the trouble of saying so?"

Masters grinned sheepishly. This had been his own view, but he hadn't wanted to say so in front of Bale. He was surprised that Green should ever have thought of what he had just said. In any case it was good enough for Bale. He said: "I'll recommend manslaughter. That means I'll have to see the Chief Constable tonight. Can you deal with that chap March?"

When Bale had gone, Hill and Brant brought March in.

"At last," said March. "What the hell d'you think you're playing at, Masters?"

Masters struggled to contain his anger. He said at last: "Miss Parker has been arrested for the murder of Mr Huth."

"What? Joan murdered Huth? Another police blunder."

"Sit down, Mr March."

Brant put a chair behind March, and Hill pushed him down onto it with pressure on the shoulder.

Masters went on. "Not only has Miss Parker been arrested, but I blame you for it, March."

"Me? Now what maggot's got into your brain?"

"Miss Parker thought you didn't know she was Huth's mistress."

"I didn't."

"Don't lie to me, March. I'm not in the mood for it. Any man can afford to get married on the salary paid to a manager at Barugt. But you had to wait for a Controller's salary. Why?"

"I don't know what you're blathering about."

"Because you thought you couldn't compete with Huth until you had a really big salary. You were so unsure of yourself you didn't think Miss Parker would marry you until you could provide a suitable alternative to Huth's presents. You didn't think the girl would have you for yourself."

"I'll take you apart for this, Masters."

"I don't think so. You're all bluff. And gutless with it. You despised Huth but hadn't the guts to get out of his firm. You accepted everything he had to give. But you wouldn't tell Miss Parker the one thing that would have made her happy and saved her from getting into this mess. Why the blazes didn't you tell her you knew she was Huth's mistress?"

212

"I tell you I didn't know."

"Didn't you? Right. Salary apart, why did you choose her and her alone to listen to your ravings against Huth? Because you were frightened you'd lose your job if anybody else at Barugt knew? Or because you couldn't think of a better way to make her break with him?"

March leaned forward. "You're raving," he said. "I loved Joan. I asked her to marry me."

"I notice you used the past tense. Perhaps you didn't mean to. We shall see. You can prove what you think about her. I hope you'll only have three years to wait before you can marry her."

March stared hard. "Three years?"

"I hope no more than that. Doesn't the idea please you?"

March said nothing.

"I see. The idea of marrying a girl who will have paid a very high price to try and preserve your happiness doesn't appeal to you now. Is that it? Or are you hoping she'll get a life sentence to get you out of an awkward situation?"

March said: "No. No, that's not it at all."

"What is it, then? Tell me."

"Tell you? Why should I tell you? What's my private business got to do with the police?"

"A lot. Miss Parker asked for you because she's miserable. I promised her she should see you tonight. I was hoping you would persuade her to send for a solicitor."

"I don't know any solicitors."

"I do. Some very good ones."

March said nothing.

Masters said: "Well, what do you say? Do you want their addresses?"

Still March said nothing.

Masters said quietly: "I should get out now, Mr March,

213

while the going's good. If I have to look at you much longer I might lose my temper."

Hill put a hand under March's arm, yanked him to his feet and propelled him towards the door.

Green said quietly: "That poor lass isn't going to like this. I hope Sergeant Hill helps that bastard down the front steps with his boot."

Masters looked at him for a moment. He said, almost automatically, "Thanks, Greeny." He walked the floor for a few moments. "She won't listen to me, and I don't think she'll do any more for any of you. But somebody's got to see her." Then he picked up the phone, dialled, and spoke for a short time.

Twenty minutes later Mrs Huth limped in.

"Where is that poor girl, Mr Masters?"

Masters said: "It was very good of you to come."

"No need to thank me. I'll go straight to her. I'll call you if I want you."

Green said: "You can't let *her* into the cell."

Mrs Huth turned to him. "I assure you I shan't try to wreak revenge on her. She needs help. Her fiancé has deserted her. That's bad enough. But it was my husband who brought her here. I must do all I can to put that right. I think I can do a lot. At any rate I'm going to try."

Masters took her arm and escorted her out of the office.

By the year 2000, 2 out of 3 Americans could be illiterate.

It's true.

Today, 75 million adults...about one American in three, can't read adequately. And by the year 2000, U.S. News & World Report envisions an America with a literacy rate of only 30%.

Before that America comes to be, you can stop it...by joining the fight against illiteracy today.

Call the Coalition for Literacy at toll-free **1-800-228-8813** and volunteer.

**Volunteer
Against Illiteracy.
The only degree you need
is a degree of caring.**

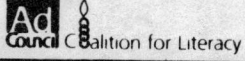

Ad Council Coalition for Literacy